PRIVILEGED LOVE

BLAZIN' LOVE BOOK TWO

JA'NESE DIXON

PUBLISHING

Blazin' Love (Contemporary Romance)

Platinum Love (Book 1)

Privileged Love (Book 2)

Exclusive Love (Book 3) [Coming April 2019]

Steamy Sensations Holiday Love

[for St. Patrick's Day]

ISBN-13: 978-1-950405-03-9 (paperback)

Printed in the United States of America.

CONTENTS

SNEAK PEEK: ROCKSTAR SECRETS

**3 wishes... 2 reluctant hearts...
1 steamy St. Patrick's Day!**

It's St. Patrick's Day.

The day is really not important, at least that's what I thought. I dress to impress, ready to secure my first contract as a partner with Platinum Prestige.

Simple, right? No, I wish.

I'm Harper Price. I've joined my best friends in starting an elite concierge service and I'm up. My sole task is to lease an airplane from Liam.

I walk in, he proposes, I walk out.

Apparently, his billions have gone to his head and now the sexy, arrogant menace won't leave me alone. His head is hard as a brick. (Take that any way you want.) And he refuses to accept "no" in any language. But I'm done with love.

No more.

Nada.

No mas.

Yet secretly, I'm scribbling my first name with his last name. Then he whispers, "Live a little Harper." And his money green eyes shine like dollars signs as he throws an unexpected curve ball. He'll grant three wishes, when…not if…I say yes.

Does having the most eligible rich bachelor begging to put a ring on it make me lucky? Hell no!

Not when my heart is screaming leap, my head is screaming caution, and my panties are.…

Oh hell, this is a f'in plane crash waiting to happen.

What is a woman to do?

"**J**erk!" I thrust the wine across the table in true reality show grandeur. I watch the wine slide down his face and trickle down his chin. The pool of red gathering on his white shirt is the only satisfaction I'll have after another night of watching him appraise every woman in the room with lust-filled eyes.

Marcel's head snaps in my direction, the lust traded for anger. He reaches for a napkin. "What is wrong with you, Harper?"

"You're what's wrong with me." I stand up, pushing away from the table. "Why did you bring me to this fancy Mongolian restaurant to behave like a snake? I'm done with tonight, and I'm done with you."

"Stop being a brat."

I turn to leave, and Marcel grabs my wrist. I yank it free, pulling my balled hand to my side. I want to drive my itty-bitty fist through his wandering eyes. It's who he is, and I can't fault him for that.

This is my fault. I thought I was different. I knew he had a way with women and he insisted that he change. I thought our chemistry was enough. That our history was enough. But once again my natural slant towards giving him the benefit of the doubt, blocked my judgment.

I smooth my hands over my dress, pulling my shoulders back. "Lose my number."

"Gladly." Marcel wipes his face. The man is fine, a beautiful brown masterpiece, and he knows it. But he's a goliath bullfrog, an oversized, slimy reptile. I take that back. That's insulting to reptiles. Yet here I am.

Again.

I stomp through the restaurant making sure he sees what he'll miss. I'm a few inches over five feet, but I don't give a damn. Thanks to a standing appointment with my trainer, my full hips, snatched waist, and round, natural butt make for a sight coming and going. So, I envision my best Beyoncé fan, tossing my hair over my shoulder winking at the many admirers as I make my grand exit in slow motion, pretending my heart isn't crushed.

I reach the door, giving Marcel a parting glance. So much for speed dating. I mentally scratch that one off my list along with Marcel. I've tried dating apps, blind dates, and my mother sprinkled in the sons of all her besties. But I'm still single.

I step outside looking up at the dark sky. Suddenly the clouds crack open. The downpour covers me plastering my white dress to my body. I'm officially done with tonight. I pull off my shoes quickly shuffling to my car through the rain.

I yank open the door, thankful I don't need a key. I plop down and open my visor. I'm drenched. I'm pissed. Then a scream escapes from the pit of my soul.

"That's it!" I pull open my armrest and find some tissues to dry my face. "No more, Harper. You can't keep doing this to yourself." I dry my face, but for some reason, I can't control the tears flowing from my eyes. No more playing nice, it hurts too much.

"Suck it up, Harper."

But I'm not listening. I grab my cellphone from my clutch. I text the guys, *SOS. S&J ASAP.* I turn on the sound for my phone then toss it into a cupholder. I finish drying my face, and my phone is singing a melody of hope from my guys.

I tap the first text from Hunter, *Roger that.*

I'm there, from Charlee makes me chuckle. I know she'll be late, but I never doubt that she will be the one cussing and fussing the loudest.

The others roll in, and I smile, grateful for amazing friends. All nine confirmed.

I'm knocking on thirty's door, and my biological clock is ticking louder since watching Hunter walk down the aisle with Ben. I'm happy for her, but I can't help but wonder, *When will I find Mr. Right?*

Not Mr. Right Now. Not Mr. I Want You And Your Girlfriends Too.

I pull out my emergency makeup kit and try to repair the damage thanks to the rain. Dudes now days have too many options. I close the compact glancing down. Next, I need to fix my outfit, but I don't want to drive all the way home. *Target.*

I turn the key in the ignition, minutes later I swoop into a parking space and run inside, praying my see-through dress doesn't give some old man a heart attack. I quickly find jeans and a boyfriend t-shirt. I leave on my heels, and I toss the beautiful white dress into the nearest trashcan. Last is my now frizzy hair. I gather it up into a messy bun, and I'm pleased with my reflection.

"Thatta girl." I tuck my black clutch under my arm.

I walk out of Target back to my car feeling like myself. Minutes later I park outside Smith & Jameson with time to spare. I apply some gloss, staring into my eyes realizing, I'm a frog magnet.

I'm talking about slimy, sleazy, and green. I'm drawing these ultimate losers from the pond, and I can only deduct that I'm the common factor. That *I* attract losers.

I search my eyes looking for it, hoping to see the thing *they* see in me. And all I see is, Harper, a woman that goes hard for her friends and family. I'm loyal and give one thousand percent because my parents taught me life gives you what you need when you need it. So, maybe life is speaking and telling me I don't need it. I don't need love. Not that kind of love, at least.

For as long as I can remember, I've always wanted the *when two become one* in life. To be someone's rib, his ride-or-die. To be a wife and a mother.

Call me old fashion. Call me crazy. Call me a princess,

trying to find a prince, hence the scattered toads around my otherwise perfect life.

I flip the visor closed and head towards the restaurant, tardiness is not my style. And like the change of seasons and time, maybe it's time I find a new version of Harper Anne Price.

I *was* that girl. But now I need to give this restless heart of mine a break. Because one thing I know for sure, I'm done kissing frogs.

～

*T*wo drinks in and I'm mellow. The guys are talking all at once, and Hunter leans over whispering, "Ready to talk?"

I shrug, signaling the waiter for drink number three. "I'm officially off the market."

"You found a Boo?" Charlee perks up across the table.

"No."

"Oh." Her face goes long. "Harper, who did what *now*?"

"I went out with Marcel."

"I told you that guy is a first-class jerk," Parker says, her face bunched up in disgust. "All he dates are heiresses."

"Leech." Taylor sucks her teeth.

"Well, I do have the name and the bank account. But I thought… I honestly don't know what the hell I thought." I take a sip of my wine. "I've known him since high school. We dated before he realized how fine he is and he actually was a nice guy. Once upon a time."

"*Was* is the key word in that sentence," Hunter adds. "Sweetie, you're too nice. You give men *waaaaayyyyy* too much credit."

"I need to school you about these dudes." Charlee leans forward, class is in session. She props her elbow on the table holding up a finger. "First, you need to stop thinking every dude is husband material, because *he ain't*. Second, you need to stop thinking every dude will appreciate wifey material, because *he won't*. And lastly, stop ignoring your gut. You think you attract frogs, well stop ignoring their spots."

Anxiety is bubbling in my stomach as the guys nod in unison. I don't agree, but that could attribute to the caliber of men I attract.

"People change every day. Why is it wrong, or naive, to expect the best first instead of the worst about a person? Why can't a guy say what he wants and mean it?"

"Because this ain't no damn Disney movie." Charlee lays out the harsh truth.

"That is so depressing." I shake my head, draining my glass of wine dry. Then I push it away since I'm driving tonight. "I hear you, Charlee, I'm retiring my glass slippers. No more nice Harper." I say the words but it feels like a part of my dream is dying. "Can we please change the subject? On a much better note, I want to take a more active roll in Platinum Prestige."

Hunter started an elite concierge service, all the women around the table hold a percentage. But for the most part, Hunter and her husband Ben handle everything. The guys—Charlee, Parker, Chase, Taylor, Payton, Alex, Ryann, Jordan, and I—supply our family connections, funding, and social juice. Oh, and we look damned good in our Men in Black suits—dubbed GIB, *Guys in Black*. We initially bonded over our male first names, now we're connected by our friendship, sisterhood, and business.

"What do you have in mind? I have a very ambitious list of tasks I'd like to complete before having the babies." I rub Hunter's belly beneath the table ready to be an aunt. She leans over against me, and we have a small moment. I'm close with all the guys, but Hunter is the one I call when life throws me a sucker punch, like today. And Charlee when I need the unadulterated truth.

"How can I help?" I ask.

"Me too," Charlee and several of the guys say at once.

Hunter pulls out her cellphone sitting upright. This is what I need to stop thinking about what I expected from my life by my thirtieth birthday. I work, not because I have to, but because I want to and it would be cool to help Hunter build this majority Black women-owned brand with my best friends.

"We've secured adequate funding, but now we need to extend our line of services." Hunter glances around the table.

"What types of services?" I ask.

"Envision anything you'd want or need. Our target is people like us. Affluent, used to getting what they want when they want it. But then I want us to take it up a notch. Luxury, access, elite."

"Sign me up." Charlee squeals.

"You're already signed up, crazy woman." I nudge her with my shoulder, and we laugh. "What do we need to do?"

"Grab your phones." We all do. "Anybody and everybody you know should become a potential contact for Platinum Prestige. They should link us to various services and products. I figure we have one year to assemble our contacts before we sign up more clients."

"Are there particular connections you want to start with?" I scroll through my phone. "Because we could create an in-house database."

"How about I handle that? I can make it searchable and cataloged by services or products," Taylor says with her fingers gliding over her phone adding notes.

"Now we're talking." Hunter smiles turning to me. "Harper, I want to start with leasing a corporate jet. You think your dad could get us a meeting with Walsh Executive Jets?"

"Yeah sure." I add a note to my phone. My family's claim to Texas fame is in agriculture. We have several large ranches around the state and Dad flies between them several times a month, instead of buying a jet, we lease from WEJ.

"What about me?" Charlee asks.

"You have major connections with restaurants, foods, and services. How about you work on a list of luxury brands and start with that? I'm thinking chocolates, wines, flowers."

Charlee nods. The focus on her face makes me geeked. We are really doing this.

"And Jordan, I need you to start working on the app. We need something within the next four to six months. We can test the services on a few of our celebrity clients before rolling out next year."

For the next hour, Hunter conducts a meeting in S&J like we're in a corporate office. Every guy has her task. We have our lawyers on standby for negotiations. All we have to do is secure the meetings. Hunter and the suits will handle the details.

We schedule the follow-up meeting for next week. I take a deep breath. This is what I need to use up some time and make a shift in my life. And it sounds easy enough. *How hard could it be?*

"I'll get Ben to reserve the VIP room for us next time," Hunter says as we're closing out.

"How are the current contracts going?" I ask as we right the tables, pushing the chairs underneath. We signed Rockstar Entertainment and Smith & Jameson already. They are testing the few services we offer now.

"Great. We've scheduled event locations, delivered food. That's why I know we need a plane in our back pocket."

"I'm on it." I send a quick text to my dad, and he responds within seconds. "I'm out. Dad is actually in town. I can get my part rolling this week. We're about to kill it!"

"Damn right," Hunter says with the confidence and swagger of a true boss.

"Love you guys!" I head out to my car. I think about the guys, specifically Hunter. We all were sort of aimless before she created this idea. And now, I can't imagine her not running Platinum Prestige.

That's what I want. I want to stand up for myself in this world and contribute equally to building our business.

Time for me to boss up and shift my life in a new direction.

"You're fired." I turn back to the proposal in my hands. "Leave the notes and your building access card with Glenda."

"Liam, you're an asshole." Her face is beet red.

"I've been called worse. And it's Mr. Walsh." I drop the document on my desk. "I don't have time to waste. You are incompetent, and apparently, you believe I run a dating service." At least she has the decency to look ashamed. "Thank you for your contribution to WEJ. Now, please excuse me, I have another appointment." I push the intercom button on the phone. "Next."

The sixth event planner in less than a year drags out the door. I blame the *Austin's Most Eligible Bachelors and Bachelorettes* list. It brought in many new executive contacts but also women from every corner of the world. Who has time to read such lists? Let alone use them as their personal matchmaker.

"I told you not to do it. But would you listen to me?

No. All those degrees and the fumes of money have scrambled your common sense."

"Not today, Glenda." I write notes across the contract I'm reviewing with the necessary revisions. Then I pass it to her. "Make these changes for tomorrow's meeting."

"Don't give me that look, Liam Walsh. My letter of resignation is final. You have to stop plowing through event planners. You're too hard and expect too much."

"Is that your verdict, oh wise one?"

Glenda is my oldest employee, and she thinks she's the boss. I don't have the heart to remind her that I'm the one who signs the checks around here, including hers.

"No my verdict is, you need to get laid and stop trying to send the rest of us to the nut house. This is a job for most people, and that's normal, Liam. Don't expect us to work a million hours because you do. We have lives, *thank you* very much."

I gasp, my mouth dropping open. "What do you know about getting laid?"

"You have one more old lady joke, and Imma go upside your head." Her hardy laugh sends me over the edge laughing.

"What am I going to do without you?" I ask her thankful for the comic relief.

"You'll be rich and alone, Mr. Walsh." She drops into the chair across from me. "I took this job because I told your mother I'd look after you. But there is more to life than these four walls. Stop building WEJ long enough to build a life."

I look away from her probing eyes and somber tone.

Glenda and my mother were best friends. Her retiring is like losing my mother all over again.

"Then I'll be rich and alone," I joke despite her bleak prediction. "Will you add that to my schedule?"

"I don't know why I fool with you boy." She snatches the contract from my hand stomping out of my office. I hear her mumble, "Asking what I know about getting laid." Then she yells, "More than you apparently."

"And set up interviews with more event planners for this afternoon," I call out hearing every word of her warning. WEJ first and the rest will happen when it's time.

"I'm going to lunch."

I hear her huffing and puffing. The slam of her desk drawer means she's grabbing her purse. I glance at my watch, she'll be back in five...four...three...two...

"Do you want something from the deli?"

"Yes, *please*." I mock a bashful expression, and she flicks a dismissive hand my way.

I laugh as she mumbles and marches out of my office. The moment our suite goes quiet I realize I'm losing her. *What am I going to do without Glenda?* Her husband passed away a few years ago, and I am her final tie to Austin. Then her daughter gave birth to her first grandchild, and after spending six weeks in Nashville, Glenda is ready to move back home. I get it, but she's leaving enormous shoes to fill.

Glenda joined my staff after I kept changing executive assistants. It was driving me mad, and after complaining to my mother, she convinced Glenda to come out of retirement until I got it all worked out. That was ten years ago.

She calls BS, and she tells me what's on her mind at all times. It's annoying and endearing because I know she's here because she wants to see me reach my goals. She wants to see WEJ dominate the industry.

Trying to find a replacement is making my hair turn gray. The agency keeps sending these young women who think I'm on the menu or that they'll find a way closer to my heart and my billions. But those assumptions have earned them first class tickets out of Walsh Executive Jets. Marriage is not on my menu or radar. Scratch that. Marriage is possible.

My mother always said, "You'll know her when you see her." But I don't have time. Building a first-class aircraft leasing company from the ground up is no small feat. I'm known domestically. My next major hurdle is to establish my presence in the international market. Hence, the WEJ International Aircraft Roundtable and my need for a planner.

I rock in my chair thinking of potential options. I believe this conference will singlehandedly boost WEJ into the stratosphere, but not if I can't get through the damn thing without *wifing* the event planner.

I know how to bend the universe to accommodate my needs. Except I've seemed to misplace my mojo. Business burnout is snapping at my heels, but success waits for no man, including me. So I work nonstop, after this conference I can take time off before Glenda leaves me with yet another vital role to fill in my organization.

"Why?" I call out closing my eyes, letting my head fall back.

"Why what?" My eyes snap open and in the doorway is an unfamiliar face. A zap of awareness singes up my spine. She smiles, and I pull at my ear to disrupt the sound of singing. Because I know angels don't reside in my head.

"Who are you? And why are you in my office?" I scrub my tired eyes with the pads of my fingers. Clearly, my exhaustion has me delusional.

"I'm Harper Price, and I called out, but no one answered. Your assistant must have stepped away. I have an appointment with…"

I blink to clear my vision. She's turning the pages in a black planner. The curve in her hips fills the doorway and her black pantsuit. Full breast, wide hips, and her brown skin remind me of cinnamon. I have a million tasks to complete but watching her is more compelling.

"I'm sorry," she says with a soft smile.

"Sure take your time," I say a little harsher than I intend. The furrow in her brow and spark in her eyes make me almost crack a smile.

"Here it is. I'm meeting with Mr. Walsh."

"Wonderful. How can I help you?" I extend a hand to the chairs in front of my desk, sitting forward. I like the jolt I feel from her obvious annoyance with my responses. "Price?" I turn the name over in my mind as she sits in front of me. "As in James Price, the rancher?"

"Yes." Her back stiffens. "He's my father."

"So, you had *Daddy* call in a favor? Gotta love

nepotism." I want to see her eyes shoot lightning again. This time I swear I hear a growl. *She's a feisty one.*

"My father offered to connect us concerning a business matter."

"I'm listening."

"I'm here representing..." She takes a deep breath glancing down at her hands. She's nervous. I usually like having this effect on people. But at this moment I feel her pain as she clears her throat. "I am here to discuss a business matter." She freezes again. I can see her shaking from here.

"Look I don't have all day."

"I'm a partner with Prestige...Platinum Prestige and we would like to...lease a plane." She exhales as if it took every ounce of her energy to say that sentence.

"How long have you been in business?"

"Less than a year."

"Then no. I can't help you." I turn to my computer set on working. "Leasing a private plane is a luxury item for most businesses, especially a new business. It's a risk I'm not willing to make." I can see her fuming from my peripheral vision. She stands slowly walking to the door.

I glance over appreciating the view of her from the back. She steps out then turns around. "That's it?"

"Yes, that's it." I see light crack in her dark brown eyes. "Now, if you'll excuse me. Oh, and tell your father I'll see him at golf on Saturday."

"Tell him yourself," she says beneath her breath.

"Excuse me?"

"Tell. Him. Yourself." Her hands are on her hips. This is the most excitement I've had all day.

"Well, aren't you Daddy's pampered princess?"

"And aren't you an arrogant ass?" It drips from her tongue like acid, and I want to sample the cherry red from her plump lips.

"No, I'm a busy man with little time to waste on your little project. I have *real* businesses waiting to lease my jets."

"We are a *real* business."

"And they sent you?" I chuckle. Yes, she's beautiful, curvy, and her smooth skin looks as soft as rose petals. But she has distraction written all over her.

"You know what? Screw you."

"Name the day and time princess."

"You wish jackass!"

Harper stomps out of my office, and I sit staring at the space she occupied. I'm torn between the compulsion to follow her and the need to understand what just happened.

Catch her, a voice commands and I'm stunned. My heart slows to a crawl.

"You know what..." She's back. Now, I'm impressed. *Feisty indeed.* "I don't appreciate you taking my nervousness for us being a joke. We are a legitimate business with real clients ready to utilize *your* services. Hunter has worked hard to secure RSE and S&J, and we could help *your* business. But you'd rather act like a di—"

"Hunter Preston...?"

"Of course you'd latch on to her name you slimy leech. I'm out of here. Have a good day, loser."

She stomps out again this time with Glenda over her shoulder. "Hire her."

"What? You have really lost your mind, besides she's not here for a job." I don't want to hire her, that woman is my wife. I take a deep breath keeping that thought to myself. Then Glenda steps directly in front of me, blocking my view.

"The woman has a planner in her hands and balls bigger than most men. Hire. Her."

"Who are you?" I stare at her. She said balls like it's a natural part of our conversations.

"Go. Get. Her Liam."

I jog down the hall impressed. I would have followed her without Glenda's help. Harper is like Glenda on steroids. "Harper, wait up."

"Not in your dreams." She's pushing the elevator button with such force that I know she's pissed.

"I came to apologize."

"Do you treat everyone with such…disdain? You can't go around talking to people like that and think it's normal. I'm sorry for going off but you are such an ass—" She glances over catching herself.

"It's okay. It's not the first time I've heard it. You don't make a billion dollars from nothing without being an *ass*, Miss Price." I slip my hands into my pockets.

She looks over at me, and her eyes are searching for something. I hope she sees whatever she needs to stay. "Have a good day, Mr. Walsh. But we'll get our plane with or without you." She crosses her arms over her chest, facing the elevator doors.

"Marry me."

"Are you crazy?" Her eyes are huge, and her reaction is gasoline to the fire kindling in my stomach.

"The craziest."

"So you're in debt and want my inheritance?"

"I'm worth several billion on a bad day. So, Daddy's money is safe with me."

Her neck snaps back. "Are you really *that* mad?"

I shrug. "Yes." *Mad about you.* The chorus in my head is latching on to this fiery goddess and not letting her go.

I ran down the hall because Glenda sent me. Actually, I ran down the hall to catch Harper because I feel electricity flowing through my veins. This has never happened before. Her outright reluctance shows me she doesn't give a damn about my money, a first for me. And it makes me more curious about this woman. A woman who's nervous about pitching for a jet, but spits fire when pushed.

My mother was right. Harper Price is my wife. There's not a single doubt in my mind.

"What is it a Black girl fetish?" Her eyes squint suspiciously with an index finger wagging in my direction.

"No, but I believe I have a *Harper* fetish." She gasps, chomping her mouth closed. I smile, crossing my arms over my chest. She is beautiful with curves calling out to be caressed. I could fight with this woman all day.

"No, not on your life. I don't know you, I don't like you, and you reek privilege."

"But you're attracted to me."

"I've been attracted to much worse." The elevator dings, she steps inside. "Bye, Mr. Walsh."

"I'll see you soon, Miss Price." I watch the doors slide closed holding her eyes. *She'll be mine.*

I'm mortified. I crawled to Charlee's house with my tail between my legs. I suck at finding a man, and I apparently suck at being a businesswoman too. I can't even look at her.

"Harper, what happened? It can't be that bad." She holds open the door, and I head straight to the couch.

"It's worse." I drop, letting my purse slide off my shoulder to the floor.

"Wait, let me get a snack."

Charlee closes the door and heads to the kitchen. To keep from crying, I laugh at her and my ridiculous response to Liam. *How did I ruin the one task Hunter gave me?* And who was that vile woman in his office? I've never *ever* behaved that way in my life. I massage my temples.

"Take it from the top." I feel the couch bounce and the smell of buttered popcorn. I look over at her.

"Charlee? I'm dying, and your ass is eating popcorn."

"And you're cussing. This is gonna be *goooood*. Let me get a soda." She's off again, and I laugh until I cry. Then she returns with a Dr. Pepper in her hands.

"I can't stand you."

"Heifer, please. You love me, and you know it." She twists the top, takes a drink making a loud slurp sound. "Tell me everything."

So I do. I tell her about my awful presentation or lack thereof. And about calling Liam a jackass. But I'll keep his *fake* proposal to myself.

"Lies! I don't believe you. Did you record it?"

"No, I didn't record it. How can I record me, telling the CEO of a company *we* want to do business with, screw you?"

"How does he look?"

"What?" I shake my head in shock. Okay, maybe I should have gone to Hunter's house. But I didn't want to disturb her or tell her how I screwed up our chance of getting an airplane from WEJ.

"How does the man look? Describe him from top to bottom. Don't leave out a single detail."

I take a deep breath.

"And don't lie, Harper," she adds with a shifty look in her eyes.

"He's about, I don't know, five ten, five eleven maybe. Reddish hair, a full beard." I run my hands down my face mocking the shape.

"White?"

"Uh-huh."

"His eyes?"

I ignore the excited spike in her voice and think back. "They're green...no blue-green. They sort of changed while we were shouting."

"Shouting?"

I nod.

"Huh-huh. And his build, athletic, dad belly?"

"Where are you going with this?" I sigh, hunching over. I'm ready to stop thinking about Liam Walsh, and my epic fail.

"Don't give up on me, Harper. Keep going, this is better than I thought. His build?"

"Whatever...broad shoulders, definitely not a dad bod or belly. He's probably got a six-pack. Yeah, I'm certain. And the way his shirt pulled at his sleeves." I pick at the arm of my shirt. The man is movie star gorgeous. Model even. The way his eyes flashed blue-green like the Atlantic Ocean. I could get lost in his eyes if he didn't make me feel hot and cold, fire and ice. But I need a plane, and he has a fleet of them. I need to calm my raging reaction to him long enough to get his commitment to supply us a plane. "Charlee Raine, you are not slick!" I glance over at her. "He's not my type."

"Liar. When is the last time you felt so challenged?" Charlee laughs around a mouthful of popcorn. "And I don't have to be slick. It's written all over your face."

"What my dislike of the man?"

"No, your attraction to the man. It caught you off guard is all. Admit it, Harper."

"I will not."

"Pretty please…" She is singing please and Soul Train dancing on my last nerve. "Tell me the truth."

"I can't and I won't."

"But if you could?" Her eyebrows are wiggling.

I can't tell her this underlying rage is steeped in desire. My heart racing, blood pumping, hands sweating, and all for a man. I have to see Liam as another frog, the froggiest of frogs, not acceptable for my pond, much too slimy to touch. Even if the man is absolutely yummy.

"I don't know why I came over here."

"Because your hormones got the best of you and he pushed your buttons."

"No, because I tanked the meeting and we won't get the lease, and you have to help me fix it."

"I'll help if you tell me the truth." She leans forward and pinches her fingers together so small I can barely see the space between them. "You like him, like this much. Don't you?"

"How can I like him? He made me this nasty, foul-mouthed woman."

"But…in your defense, you stood up for yourself and your friends."

"I did." I didn't think about it like that.

"Harper, it was your first time giving a presentation. You went alone, and he threw you off by his killer looks."

"I didn't say—"

"You don't have to, I know these things." Charlee places the popcorn bowl aside. "So, after all of this shouting what did he say?"

"He asked me to marry him," I mumble.

"What?" Her eyes widen, and she's squealing and kicking her legs around. "You went from kissing toads to kissing billionaires. Oh, I have got to see *this* man."

"No, no, no. And who said anything about kissing?" I see this baby running out of control the moment she jumps up and heads to her bedroom. "Where are you going?"

"To change clothes. We're going back to WEJ, and I'm gonna to meet...your future baby daaaadddddyyyyyy." She's dancing into her bedroom, and I'm mortified. We cannot go back to Liam's office. I mumbled like an idiot and cursed like a drunken sailor. He turned me inside out while his handsome face appeared to bask in my uncomfortable state.

Liam brought out a side of me I didn't know existed. I sit back on the couch. I have to get out of going. I can't let Charlee go back, and I can't tell Hunter I failed. And I surely can't tell my Dad I called his golf partner a jackass. So much for turning my life around. I sigh, dropping my head against the cushion.

I search the ceiling, roaming until my eyes settle on the pictures from our last vacation. We had a great time in the Bahamas. I take a deep breath.

It's time to get real, Harper. Is Charlee right? Am I attracted to Liam?

Yes! The inner me is back to its frazzled state just thinking about the man. But finding an attractive man isn't my issue, finding a man open to love and ultimately marriage is. So, I can't let his dreamy eyes kill my chance at owning my role in Platinum Prestige.

Liam had me tongue-tied, and his outright dismissal hurt my feelings. They ask me to do one thing, and I tanked. Maybe I'm not cut out for business either. Then something Liam said comes to mind, *You don't make a billion dollars from nothing without being an ass Miss Price.*

I don't want to be an ass, but it felt good to stand toe-to-toe with him. To not be run over. Yes, I fumbled, but my father always says, "The first no is merely an opportunity to re-saddle and ride it again."

I always thought of it as cowboy logic. But today, it makes total sense. This was no different than getting tossed off a horse. In which case, I'd stand up, dust myself off and get right back on.

This is my chance to show myself I'm a *real* partner in Platinum Prestige and not just because Hunter is my friend. I sit up. It's time I get back on the horse.

"Charlee, I'll see you at S&J." I grab my purse.

"Nooooo." She runs into the living room half-dressed. "I'm going with you."

"I have to do this on my own. But stay near the phone, just in case he has to call security or something like that." There's a slight chance that Liam and I could combust.

"Can you please record it?"

"No! You make me so sick. I love you." I kiss her cheek.

"Love you too. And, Harper"—Charlee grabs my hands—"you can do this. Hunter always says you bring up our average. It's because you're the voice of reason, you're honest to a fault, and your heart sees the best in us all."

"I can't go in there with my soft heart."

"Yes, you can. Just be yourself." She hugs me. "I think Liam is bringing out a tougher version of you and I can't wait to meet her. Minus that nasty tongue." She wags a finger.

"Bye, Charlee and thank you." I roll my shoulders back. I'm so nervous but what do I have to lose. I freeze at the thought. "What if I fail again?"

"Just take a deep breath and speak your heart."

I nod. "What if he sets me off again?"

Charlee shrugs. "Trust your gut. As long as you don't drop an f-bomb I think it's repairable. And you have to live a little Harper." Her eyes twinkle with humor.

"Okay. I'll call you as soon as I leave." I hug her once more moving towards the door on weak legs. "And don't tell Hunter," I call back.

"I won't. Now go on, Baby Hunter." She snaps her fingers rolling her hips. "Take your cussing tail back over there and get us a jet."

"I'm not listening to you."

"You don't have to. Your vajayjay hears me and *Liam* loud and clear."

"Why do I listen to you?"

"Because where you are the voice of reason, I'm the voice of your naughty fantasies." She laughs. How does she come up with this stuff? "And I expect all the juicy details tonight."

"Charlee, you really need to find a hobby or something. See you later, love you girl." I toss a finger wave, leaving before she adds anymore of her naughty fantasies to my head. I drive back to WEJ. I sit in the car saying my spiel several times. I step out only after running through it three times without stumbling.

I walk up the wide sidewalk towards the twenty-story building. The sun is setting, and I glance at my watch. It's almost six. He's probably gone for the day.

I stop as a few people walk back towards the parking garage. I can't chicken out. If he's gone, fine. But I didn't come all this way to turn around.

You can do this, Harper.

I enter the building, signing in at the security desk. Then I head back to his suite. This time there's a woman behind the desk out front with a salt-and-pepper pixy cut and bright eyes. Wait…I saw her when I charged out earlier today.

"Hi, I'm—"

"You're Harper Price. I'm Glenda, it's nice to meet you." Her smile is warm and genuine.

I accept her outstretched hand. "Nice to meet you too. Is Mr. Walsh available?"

"Yes, head on back." She nods her head towards the closed door.

"Thank you." I take a deep breath, panic is about to get the best of me. I grip my bag like a comfort blanket and take a tentative step.

"Miss Price, his bark is bigger than his bite."

"I'm sorry, Miss Glenda, but I don't believe you." I chuckle. She laughs, and her smile makes me feel at ease. "Do you have any advice?"

"Know what you want and stand your ground."

"I think I can do that." I smile back.

"I think you can too," she says.

"Can you do me a favor?" I stare at the closed door.

"Sure."

"If we start yelling, don't call the cops. Just let us duke it out."

"Got it," she says around a hearty laugh.

I reach for the door and lightly tap it.

"Come in."

I enter. I hear him talking and realize he's on the phone. His eyes widen then blaze into mine. Heat fills my body. I focus on putting one foot in front of the other. I motion a hand towards the chair asking for permission. He nods. I sit dropping my bag beside me.

Liam is talking about gasoline prices and his eyes never leave mine. I want to look away but I can't. I'm stuck. Stuck swimming in his eyes and my body is betraying me with every single second. I grip the arm of the chair for support.

The caller is talking, and he's listening. He leans back tapping his finger as if he has a problem to solve. I slide my shoes off my feet, I have to get my body to relax and remember to breathe. But there is an invitation in his smoldering gaze that I can't deny. All I can think is *Marry me*. I took it as a joke. But he said it not in a rush and without humor. He doesn't strike me as a jokester or the comedic type. He couldn't be serious. Could he?

"Miss Price. Thank you for coming back." I blink. How'd I miss him closing out his call?

My heart is racing, and I'm scared to open my mouth.

I don't want to stutter or embarrass myself. And I don't want to…feel what I'm feeling. And I hear crazy Charlee in my head, *Take a deep breath and speak your heart.*

"I came back to apologize and to ask for a second chance." I exhale a sharp breath. I did it. Now to wait for his response.

"I'm listening." He stares back waiting in silence.

I can do this. I'm a GIB. The guys need this, and they're depending on me to get it.

"I'm new at this. And you're making me so nervous."

His eyes sweep over my face, landing on my mouth. "You can't tell me that, Harper. It's Business Negotiations 101. Never let them see you sweat."

"You've already seen me sweat and swear. And I never swear. Not really, not like earlier. But you opened your mouth, and I opened mine and out it came." I place a hand over my heart. "Wow, I feel better already. It feels good to get that off my chest."

Liam is shaking his head in disbelief, and I'm starting to feel like myself again. Then he smiles. Why did God give him the best of everything? He's rich, handsome, has beautiful teeth, a head full of hair, it doesn't seem fair.

"What are you thinking, Harper?"

"God must *really* love you." He stares at me then bursts out laughing. He laughs so long I join him until Glenda steps into the room.

"Yes, Glenda?" His eyes remain locked with mine.

"I won. I'll see you tomorrow." I send a questioning glance his way. "It was nice meeting you, Miss Price."

What's that about? I look at Glenda. "Harper, please."

"Harper, I hope to see you again soon." She says soon with such force that I look back at Liam.

"I'll see you tomorrow, Glenda," Liam says.

She waves and then we're alone.

"Continue, Harper, you have my undivided attention."

CHAPTER 4

LIAM

"*D*id you hear anything I said?" Harper asks.

I blink. "No, I apologize." I haven't been able to think straight since the elevator closed behind her and now here she is. She appears relaxed this time.

"What part did you miss?"

"All of it." I'm ashamed to admit. "I can't seem to focus with you around. Please give me the highlights." I lean forward commanding my ears to listen.

"I need to lease a plane. So instead of giving me a fast no, can you tell me what you need to reconsider?"

"I need you to help me organize a roundtable." I thought about it earlier, and it would solve two pressing issues. One, I need a planner, and two, I want Harper Price at my side. The woman that has my heart screaming *mine*.

"You want to hire us?"

"No, I want to hire *you*." Her eyes round and her kissable lips press together. She's not saying no, which means she's considering my request. I thought about my pushy offer earlier and realize I need to take Glenda's advice. Hiring Harper will give us a chance to get to know each other.

"So, if I help you plan this roundtable, you'll consider leasing a jet to us?"

"I'll consider it. But you have to pull it off."

"What makes you think I can do it?"

"Can you do it, Harper?" I search the depths of her eyes seeing determination. Earlier she fumbled but she came back, and that says a lot about her.

"Yes. Granted, I haven't organized a roundtable before. You'll have to be patient, I'm sure. Can you do that, Liam?"

"What happened to Mr. Walsh?"

"It went out the moment you called me Harper." Her slow smile is sexy as hell, and for a second I wonder if I've lost my mind. How am I going to work with her here?

"I can do it. You'll need to work here with Glenda to get caught up. The roundtable is scheduled less than six months away. Expect long hours. Is it a deal?"

"I'm off the market, Liam." Her back is stiff, closed off. But her eyes hold the same sparks from earlier.

"Are you married?"

"No."

"Dating anyone?" I smile.

"No."

"That's good to know."

"The answer is still no." Her tone is airy and low. "I'm

not here to apply for a job. I'm here about leasing a plane."

"Right. My planes, my terms." I sit back letting my words sink in. I need the luck in my Irish blood to get this woman to see what I see. "And I'll sweeten the pot for you. *When* you accept, I'll grant you three wishes."

"Three wishes for planning this roundtable of yours?" I hear the slight quiver in her voice. "What if I want to reserve a plane exclusively for Platinum Prestige for a year?" *There you go, Harper.* I love the challenge in her tone.

"I'd grant your request."

"Why, Liam?"

I search her eyes wishing I had a better answer than my gut is telling me to do it, or that my mother told me one day I'd find her. I find it ironic that I'm nearly begging Harper to take the job that my canned planners begged to keep. So to keep from coming across as an *arrogant ass*, I say, "I'm still trying to figure it out."

"Are you always so impulsive?" Her eyes squint as if suspicious.

"No, this is the first time." I smile. I plan to tilt the earth to make this woman mine. But I can't tell her. I sink farther into my seat aching to touch her ebony skin.

I see her chewing on the inside of her jaw. I remain quiet. This is a sweet deal. I'm out of my mind to propose it. But I'll do it to figure out why Harper. She's beautiful, but there's something about her.

Then out of nowhere, she says, "What does Business Negotiations 101 have to say about this type of deal?"

I drop my head to hide my smile. "Your goal is to always make the deal work for you. Bad deals pave the road to mediocrity. Fair deals, ones where all parties believe they have won, are the equivalent of finding a pot of gold, Miss Price."

Are you my reward after all I've endured?

She nods. "I'll talk with my business partners. I'll call you tomorrow with my decision."

By nature, I expect the best but plan for the worst and since most people find it hard to deliver unfavorable news face to face. "How about you meet me here at eight?"

Harper stands, tossing a bag over her shoulder. She extends a hand in my direction. I glance over at the calendar. Today is St. Patrick's Day and I'm hoping for a little luck. Don't think I've ever needed it before. My refusal to ever go back to living a life of poverty pads my resolve with enough fuel to outwork my competitors. And my resolve is the only luck I need, in business. But something tells me I'll need more to stake any claim on Harper.

"Do you believe in luck or fate?"

"I used to. But I've experienced too many broken promises and grand carriages morphing into rotten old pumpkins."

I'm sucked into her kind eyes. Those types of eyes would make her a target. Eyes filled with curiosity and wonder and heat and I want her, in every way a man could want a woman…in my life and in my bed. And this reality shakes me to my core. She'll be a delightful reward.

"I'm sorry to hear that, Harper." *Lucky me*, a little voice in my head confirms, and it's a done deal. I close her small hand in mine.

"Do you feel that?" I'm pleased when she nods. The current between us could power Las Vegas. It is unmatched. It's raw and hot and blue lightning. "Harper, I plan to get to know everything there is to know about you. Deal or not."

"I'll see you in the morning." Harper slips her hand away from mine and turns towards the door.

"You did good tonight, Harper."

She turns back, her face bright. "Thank you, Liam. Good night."

"I'll walk you out." I motion towards the door.

"That's not necessary."

"It is, especially if I have a chance at convincing you to help me."

She chuckles. "Do you ever give up?"

"Not when I want something." Her eyes betray her as they move from my eyes and settle on my mouth, causing my chest to expand.

"How about we change the subject? Tell me about this roundtable."

We walk and talk. I tell her about the roundtable at the beginning of the summer and the tasks left to do. The details are essential but her getting used to me is the goal. A man like me takes up space, I'm intense. I'm always on. My world is small, yet vast, it thrives in the details. And I want what I want when I want it. This is something Harper will have to learn about me, and in exchange, I'd gladly give my woman the world.

"This sounds like an ambitious undertaking."

"It is. But I think it's what we need to make WEJ known internationally."

We stop beside her car. "I honestly never gave all of this much thought. I assume you're competing with other private carriers for privacy, exclusivity, and flexibility. And then there's probably pricing with the commercial carriers."

"Yes, there's more, but you're on the right track." I lean against the hood. Her mind is sharp, and we haven't covered the specifics yet.

"Why would your competitors be willing to meet with you?"

"Great question. We can actually help each other. Think of it like a union. We can work together to ensure our rights are heard. There are also a few carriers that we pass business back and forth with as needed."

For a moment we're both assessing the other. "I'll let you go. I have a meeting. Thanks again for hearing me out."

"You're welcome." I scramble to think of a reason to make her stay. But I'm drowning in her eyes again. I figure it's best to let her leave since we're not at each other's throats and pacing is as important as the details. "I'll see you in the morning." I close the door behind her. "Drive safely."

Harper pulls out of the parking lot, and I'm not

confident she'll accept my proposal—either of them. I head back inside, prepared to work late. The marriage proposal slipped out, her fiery pushback had me wanting to see how far I could take it—and her. I growl to relieve the tension of waiting. I want Harper to say yes. I believe she'll say yes. Why shouldn't she? I made one hell of an offer. But I have a Plan B in motion, hence the stack of resumes I'll review just in case she doesn't return tomorrow.

I enter my office, dropping in the chair behind my desk with images of Harper sashaying off, the fullness of her hips, and the beauty of her smile. I type "Platinum Prestige" in a search engine, rolling closer to my desktop.

"What do we have here? An elite concierge service company."

The website is in maintenance mode. But the temporary visual is striking. Ten women, dressed in black suits. I recognize a couple. I press play on the trailer, and it opens with Hunter Preston with flashes of the others. Each talking about the brand, how it started, and then Harper smiles at the camera. Then my growing curiosity mixes with my simmering attraction creating a heated hunger for the lovely Miss Harper.

I submit a query in the form, curious to see how they'll respond. I close the browser with more questions than answers. Why didn't I get her number? I could always call James. I toss that thought aside. It's best to not involve her father, this is between Harper and I. The idea of pursuing and winning over Harper appeals to the man in me. I want her plain and simple. And I intend to get her.

I shake my head and realize it's best to call it a night. Might as well grab some dinner and come back early tomorrow. I can't focus, and it's all because of a curvy bombshell named Harper Price.

CHAPTER 5

HARPER

"*A*re you here for speed dating?" I smile at Yuki, the hostess and one of the owners of S&J.

"I should say no, but I'm Charlee's wingman tonight."

"You'll be all right. The ladies are sitting, and the guys are walking from table to table. Do you want to take notes?" She holds up a brochure.

"Yes, god help me if I forget to rate one of the guys for her." We share a knowing laugh. This is one of our regular hangout spots. The owners and staff know us well, and they're one of our clients. Yuki adds my name to the list and gives me a name tag.

I head to the bar ready for a shot then a glass of wine and to think about my day. Liam is at the top of my list. His sharp green eyes and reddish hair make for a striking contrast. Much like the turmoil, I'm feeling. Because for some odd reason I'm stuck on a question blurted out in the heat of the moment. *Marry me.* And the fact that he knows my father and still has the nerve to ask me,

Harper Price, to marry him, whether in jest or not says a lot about Liam Walsh.

"Uh oh, what happened?" I glance up from my daydream to find Hunter. "How'd the meeting go?"

"Uh, it went." I drain my glass dry. "How are Titi's babies?" I talk to her belly.

"Titi's babies are playing soccer." She chuckles sitting next to me. "How'd the meeting go?"

"It went. I have a followup with Liam tomorrow morning."

"Liam?" Her head snaps in my direction.

"I mean, Mr. Walsh."

"A shot and a glass of wine." She rocks side to side to get comfortable on the bar stool. "Do I want to know?"

I hate that my friends can read me like a book. "It went well. I made my request...and...and he made an offer. I..." I take a deep breath, in my nose and out my mouth. I hate when I stumble over my words. It makes me feel uncomfortable, ready to keep to myself. And I find myself wondering if people doubt my ability to interact professionally.

"Did something happen?" Her eyes squint in a motherly way.

"I swear you have the mother gaze down." I laugh.

"I do, don't I?" Hunter dances in her chair. "Girl we need to find a booth, my butt is too damn big for these stools. "There's one. Let's go over there."

"Are you going into the speed date too?"

"Girl, and have Ben drag me, and the twins, out? No,

ma'am. Charlee said she was meeting you here, so I came to check on you."

"Why?" I ask, my heart dropping.

"Why? We always debrief, and you didn't call me."

"You thought I'd blow it?" My heart sinks to a new low.

"No, Harper, or I wouldn't have asked you to do it. Why would you ask me that?"

"Because I…I don't know. It's been a rough day."

"Hey, Baby Hunter!" Charlee strolls up dressed to kill. "How'd it go?"

Her tone is way too chipper, and Hunter's eyes swing in my direction. Charlee tips her head towards Hunter in a *Tell her* gesture. I shoot back my best, *Not now!*

"I know one of y'all heifas better say something. What is it, Harper? Do I need to find Liam?" The stank she uses on his name is real.

"Hold that thought, let me get a drink." Charlee runs off.

"Imma strangle her ass." I reach for my glass, and it's empty.

"Harper Anne Price!"

"I just need a moment to process it all." I stare at the glass, not meeting her eyes. Then her hand rests on my forearm. God, I hate her and love her all at the same time. "I blew it."

"Okay." She turns in the booth seat. "We'll find another company. No biggie."

I look up. "Really?" Scratch the hate, I love her, love her.

"Yeah, we'll be the hottest company in Austin. It's his loss. Right?" She squeezes.

"No, there's more."

"Harper, you do remember that I can't drink right?" Her hand rests on her belly.

I smile. "Yes, it's not *that* bad."

"Good, tell me about it."

"And don't leave out a single detail." Charlee slides in the booth across from me.

So I tell them, everything through to him closing my car door. "What are you going to do?"

"Say no, obviously?" I look back and forth between them. These two are yin and yang.

"I don't understand what makes it so obvious." Charlee air quotes.

"I can't marry a man I don't know."

"And that's your only conundrum?" Hunter asks with a smirk.

"Exactly?" Charlee adds eating from her plate of loaded nachos.

"Either y'all are speaking another language, or I'm missing something. You think I should say yes?" I reach for a nacho, flicking off the jalapeño, and popping the cheesy goodness in my mouth.

"Do you think you should say yes?" Hunter asks grabbing a chip too.

"One of y'all heifas better go get us another plate. Because I got dinner for one, not three."

"Hush." Hunter chuckles. "I can't give advice about

where and when. I met Ben, married him, and now I'm having his babies in less than two years."

I can't look at Charlee. Her *I told you* girl face is burning a hole in my neck.

"But Ben is not Liam."

"Tell me about him. What you know, of course?" Hunter asks.

"We're opposites. He's brash and arrogant."

"And loaded," Charlee adds.

"That's not important," Hunter adds.

"But for our legendary frog kisser, it is."

"Charlee damn," I say rolling my eyes.

"You hear that," Charlee says to Hunter. "He has her cussing. If you want my opinion, I say go for it."

"You don't meet a guy and marry him. You meet a guy and kiss him. You might meet a guy and sleep with him. Where do people meet and marry the same day?"

"Vegas," they say in unison.

We share a sisterly glance and all burst into laughter. And I'm the loudest as my side aches.

"For the record, when I say go for it, I'm not saying marry him this second. But is there anything wrong with opening your mind to the possibility?" Charlee says.

"And if we're opening our minds," Hunter asks, "what would that look like? I wasn't looking for love or having babies, but it found me. I don't want to imagine where I'd be if I'd told Ben no. I wouldn't have this life. And I love my life." Her eyes fill with tears. I drop my head on her shoulder.

"What type of precautions should you have in place?"

I look at Charlee. She's the most vocal, but I see where she's going. "I mean the thought of a man bringing more money to the table doesn't shield you, but it does mean he's not a Marcel."

"I'd hope not," I say. "I think planning his roundtable would help me."

They share a glance then look in my direction.

"Y'all I'm new to all of this. You two are jumping in with two feet, and I never thought I'd be here. I never even thought about getting a job. I wanted to do charity work and raise a family. But in the few minutes of talking...or yelling, he brought something out of me."

"Like what?" Hunter leans her elbow on the table, resting her chin on her palm.

"I felt challenged and alive."

"And aroused." Charlee wiggles her eyebrows.

"Yeah, that too." I consider the pros and cons. "I could shadow him for these meetings and pick up on the way he handles clients. And he said he'd grant me three wishes once the round table is complete."

"Three wishes?" they sing.

"What does that mean?" Hunter asks.

"I don't know. But I'm thinking a year lease for us, listing Platinum Prestige as a sponsor for his roundtable, and I haven't thought of the last one." I chew on the inside of my jaw. This is sounding more promising the more I think about it.

"What if he's some deranged lunatic?" Hunter asks.

"We'll call in our resident cowboy, Mr. James Price, of course," Charlee declares.

I laugh. "He's known my dad for years."

"How old is he?"

"I'm not sure. But can't be more than thirty five." I guess.

"Whatever you decide you have my full support," Hunter declares.

"Mine too." Charlee extends a hand across the table.

I smile pleased to have them in my corner. Then a sensuous tingle runs up my spine. I glance up.

Blink. Blink. Am I imagining?

I see Liam standing at the bar. My mouth drops open, and he's staring at me with longing in his eyes.

"Is that him?"

I try to nod discreetly, but I'm not sure if my head is moving.

"Hot damn. That man is ready to eat you alive." I swear she's hollering and I'd kill her if I could move.

"I agree with Charlee."

"You can't," I whine not taking my eyes off of him. His dress shirt is unbuttoned at the neck. He appears relaxed.

"I can't what honey." Hunter is talking through her teeth with a smile stretched across her face.

"You can't agree with Charlee. She'll have me butt naked screaming the man's name in the middle of S&J."

"As if, you're not thinking about it already." Charlee waves Liam over, and I'm planning her funeral in my head.

He approaches the table, his gaze locked with mine. "Harper."

The words lodge in my throat. Why God? Why am I

either cursing the man out or a mumbling idiot? This isn't fair. Then he smiles. "Ladies."

I swear they stop breathing, and so do I. He is that *fine*.

"Join us," Hunter offers sliding over. I turn throwing pin-sharp daggers at her with my eyes. She shrugs.

"I have a few minutes while I wait on my food." Liam sits next to me. He fills the space, his leg rests against mine. His eyes turn blue-green unsettling me.

Uh-hum. Charlee clears her throat. But I can't pull my eyes away.

Liam drapes an arm across the back of the booth leaning closer. "Aren't you going to introduce me to your friends?" He pulls back with a mischievous smile on his face.

"You're enjoying this, aren't you?" Breathing and thinking is a chore right now.

"Enjoying your leg against mine, the smell of your perfume, the feel of your—" His hand is on my thigh, and I jump. A smile is tugging on the corners of his lips.

"Liam, these are my best guys." I glance at them. "Hunter and Charlee."

He leans over me shaking their hands, brushing his body against mine.

"I'm going to get you for this," I whisper for his ears to hear.

"Promise?" He settles beside me, and it feels like he's done it a million times.

"So, Liam, since you got my girl all hemmed up. Tell us about yourself."

I roll my eyes up to heaven. *If I've ever done anything right in this life, help me. Please control Charlee's tongue.*

"That won't work. But I think you should change your mind," Liam says.

"About what?"

"Fate?" I'm frozen in time, and his attention is locked on me, as he said earlier, I had his undivided attention, and it feels incredible.

"We're being extremely rude right now," I counter loving the way we play.

Liam flashes his dazzling smile. "I'm sure your *guys* are ear hustling."

I burst out laughing, and my defenses begin to subside. Is it wrong to bask in this moment? To let myself feel what I feel because it feels good?

"I like that."

"What?"

"Your smile. And your attitude is sexy as hell too."

"Liam!"

"Let me take you out."

"Take me out?" I'm speechless. He shows no signs of relenting. And I honestly don't want him to. I feel a slight nudge from Hunter. "And what about your proposal?"

"Which one?"

"Liam?"

"I'm just making sure we're on the same page." He shrugs, and I'm not buying it. "But both still stand."

"Both?" *I can't breathe.*

"Both."

I pull my lip between my teeth and chew. He is

disrupting my night of thinking. He is oozing take me to bed vibes. And I am falling for it. I feel it, and I'm not sure if I like it.

Liam leans forward, his lips brushing my ear. "Live a little. Go out with me. I'll show you that your doubts are unfounded."

"And if they are?"

"They're not." His smile is rubbing off on me.

"You're awful confident." And it's knocking at the door of my heart. *Can I trust him?*

"I know." I roll my eyes. There's only one way to find out. I'll accept his offer to work on the roundtable. To see him up close and personal will show that I'm right about declining his *other* proposal. I glance over his arm behind me, his hard body beside me, and I feel softer towards him. I just can't tell him. His head would probably explode.

"You do know fighting is futile?" I shake my head. *This man.*

"Says who?" I challenge.

"Says me."

CHAPTER 6

*H*arper is as stubborn as I'm confident she'll come around. Her constant refusal had me tossing and turning. And I never toss and turn. But I did last night after hanging out with Harper and her friends. Another thing I haven't done since grad school, just sitting around laughing, talking, seeing Harper through the eyes of her *guys*.

I enter my office before four o'clock. I couldn't sleep so I might as well get ahead of my day. Today, my schedule is stretched to capacity. I have my regular tasks and the event planner duties, which call for meeting with caterers.

Lucky me. Glenda can help, but I need her to manage the office.

I remove my jacket, sitting behind my desk. All systems are on, and I'm in the zone. I make calls, review documents. Sign contracts, drink coffee like it's a lifeline. Then a soft knock stops me. It's her.

The woman who kept me awake last night. The woman who finds it so easy to tell me no, in every way imaginable. The woman who exudes a level of peace, even when she's shaking with nervousness. The woman who has me damn near begging to make her mine and I honestly can't figure out why. But my heart knows she's it and I trust myself knowing the details will come when they're needed.

Harper is a spitfire. I barked, growled, and yelled yet she turned right back around, scared and all.

"May I come in?"

"Absolutely." I sit the contract I'm reading on the desk, stopping to appreciate the view.

Harper has curves in all the right places. Her hair falls over her shoulders in shiny black waves. Her black suit from yesterday is replaced by a cream body-hugging dress. *How am I going to concentrate?*

"Liam, you can't look at me like that all day."

I smile. "Like what, Harper?"

"You know what I mean." She sits in the chair across from me.

"I know, but I want to hear you say it." I lean forward.

"Let me close the door." She pops up, and the curve of her ass has my hands itching to caress it. "There you go again."

"Look you might as well pluck my eyes out because I can't help it."

"Are you a gawker? Is that what you do?"

"A gawker? What the hell?"

"A guy who watches every ass, hollers at every chick.

Is that you?" She pulls a planner out of her bag dropping it on her lap with a deep sigh. Her shoulders slump a little. Then her eyes search mine.

"You're serious?"

"Dead ass."

"And that's yes?"

"Stop playing, Liam. I admit I'm attracted to you. But I'm done with men like you. I'll accept your offer to help with the roundtable. But—"

"Did I look at a single woman other than you last night?"

"No, but—"

"Who was I with?"

"Me. But, Liam—"

"Who was I damn near begging, last night?" My voice echos off the walls. This woman is crawling beneath my skin, and I can't take it.

"Me." Her voice is a whisper.

"How about you stop comparing me to the lame ass guys you dated before?" A muscle quivers in my jaw. The silent standoff is thick with sexual tension and contaminated with her past. And judging by the hard expression on her face I've managed to piss her off *again*.

"What would you like for me to do today?"

"Harper."

"Liam, I'm here to work." She opens her planner, making sure our eyes don't meet.

"Walk with me." I grab my jacket. I'm too tired to have this conversation and coddle her feelings. "We're meeting with caterers through lunch." I stop by Glenda's desk. "Take care of my calls and reschedule my meetings."

"Liam." Glenda places a hand on mine. Her eyes pleading. "Be patient," she whispers darting a glance towards Harper. She squeezes before pulling away. "I'll take care of it."

I take a deep breath. "Thank you."

I know I'm rough around the edges. But I'm not gaming Harper. I've never had someone challenge my integrity, let alone do it in my face. We stop in the conference room. I open the door standing back ensuring no part of my body touches hers.

I have to control my eyes, and my thoughts, and my intense feelings all with no sleep. I turn my head to the ceiling. *Stick with safe topics* and get the hell out of dodge the moment the meetings are over. This plan is shoddy, but it's all I have.

"The roundtable is a total experience. I want them to leave wowed and begging to partner with WEJ. Food, venue, hotel. All of it is included. Nothing but the absolute best."

Harper is turned towards me. Her face is intense. "Do you have a particular theme in mind?"

"No. I know I don't want the same old boring box lunches or grilled chicken with green beans. I want every touchpoint to be an experience with WEJ."

"Do you have dietary concerns?"

"I'm not sure about that."

"We can create a survey and send to attendees." She opens her planner and writes a few notes. "How many people are registered? Is registration still open? Are any of the caterers connected with the venue? Sit down or buffet?"

The next thirty minutes Harper is shooting questions like a marksman. She's asking questions I didn't consider, and I can't recall having this conversation with the other planners.

The companies roll in and roll out. By the time we reached the last few Harper is running the entire conversation. We have one meeting left, and I peek down at her notes. She has pages of them. There are little stars and asterisks. And to think I doubted her. She's proven her worth in the last few hours of sifting through all the people, menus, and details of feeding these people.

"Thank you, Harper." I place a hand over hers, hearing a quick intake of her breath. I pull my hand away. "I apologize."

"You're welcome, Liam."

"Liam, your final meeting is with Luxe Cuisine," Glenda announces.

We stand, and a statuesque woman enters the conference room. "Mr. Walsh, I'm Lydia Hamilton."

"Nice to meet you, this is Harper Price our event coordinator and liaison." The title stuck after the first meeting. This would give me a clean escape when I'm ready to pass the tasks off.

"Harper."

I notice the curt tone, and apparently, Harper does too, her eyes slip towards me as we retake our seats.

I nod in Harper's direction allowing her to take the

lead. The questions are the same as before except Lydia is directing all of her answers to me. And the more she blatantly ignores Harper the more I'm ready to toss the rude woman out.

"What is your specialty, Miss Hamilton?"

"I prepared a few custom menus featuring clients' favorites." She pulls out several printed menus passing them to me. This earns her the signature Harper eye roll.

"Miss Hamilton *we* appreciate your time." I slide the menus back across the table, planting my hand on the table prepared to see this obnoxious woman out when Harper's hand rests on mine. I freeze.

"I got this," she whispers, and I fall back in my seat.

"Miss Hamilton, you're about to lose a hundred thousand dollar contract for your company, and the potential of future contracts. Is that your intent for this meeting?" The cut in her tone sends ice water down my spine. If I hadn't asked her to marry me, I'd ask her a million times right now.

"Well…no." She snaps her mouth shut.

"Then I suggest we conduct ourselves in a manner that shows you want to work with WEJ. Shall we?"

"Yes, Miss Price."

The rest of the meeting went without issue.

"Thank you for your time, Miss Hamilton, we'll be in touch." Harper stands, and I do too. The moment Miss Hamilton leaves the room Harper spins in my direction.

"Liam, you can't bark orders at people."

"Actually, I can. This is a major opportunity. People have to want it, or they'll squander it."

Harper chuckles shaking her head. "What am I going to do with you?"

"Marry me."

"Liam have a seat." I gladly sit next to her. "Why are you eager to get married? Do you have an inheritance to gain?"

"No." I smile.

"Lose a bet?"

"Nope. Not my thing."

She chews the inside of her jaw as if totally focused. "Then I don't get it."

"What is there to get? It's you, Harper. You're the reason, and I plan to ask you every chance I get."

"You do know this could be considered sexual harassment?"

"Do you feel harassed?"

"No."

"Then it's a moot point."

"Impossible," she mutters.

"I'm just waiting for you to believe that it's impossible to change my mind." I lean forward. Harper handled the meetings in record time. Seeing her in action turned me on in the hottest way. Who knew Harper in her zone would be so damn hot? "You're sexy as hell. Do you know that?"

She stares at me for a long time. "Do women come on to you like that all the time?"

"No. I don't know. I guess." I shrug. I know she's referring to Lydia Hamilton. "Do you plan to change the subject every time I compliment you?"

"You mean every time you hit on me. Yes." She closes her planner. "And what type of answer is that? Yes or no Liam. Do they?"

"Here lately yes. But not normally, at least as far as I know."

"What changed lately?"

"I was featured as one of Austin's most eligible bachelors. Want to grab some lunch?"

"Of course you are," she mumbles. "No, I need to run a few errands."

"I'll join you. We can stop and pick up something to eat while we're out." I leave the conference room with her calling my name. "Glenda, we're heading out. Want me to bring you something back?"

"Maybe. Call me when you decide." She follows me into my office. "How'd it go?"

"You're right. She's good. We finished the interviews. I think we have a winner in the bunch. Now if we can nail it down this week, I'll be ecstatic."

"How did *she* do?" She glances towards the door. I did too not seeing Harper.

"Great."

"Yay! Now, your job is to *not* run her off. Now get going."

I shake my head. "Glenda."

"Time is ticking, Liam. Now skedaddle." She pushes me towards the door, and I head back to the conference room.

"I'm ready. Where are we going?"

"Shopping for Hunter's baby shower gift."

CHAPTER 7

HARPER

hy am I really saying no? I consider as I watch Liam search through baby clothes. He is having too much fun on this shopping trip. I thought he'd run for the hills and again this man surprises me.

"What is it, sweetheart?" The endearment bursts through another barrier.

"I can't keep fighting off your advances. We have to come to some middle ground here."

His sinister smile makes me ache. "I told you."

"Yeah, yeah, yeah. You told me. Now make it stop."

"There's only one way." He places a handful of decorated onesies in my basket. Then stops in front of me. "Say yes."

"I can't," I whisper. And I can't tell him I'm scared shitless of the feelings I'm feeling. I can't say I want to throw caution to the wind, scream yes, and experience a new type of normal with him. I can't because it is insane to meet a man, fall in love, and marry him after two days. *I can't!*

"But you can. Just say the word." His confidence should hold a patent.

"How can you be so sure?"

"Who is actually certain of anything in life? Nothing is what it seems. Nothing is what we expect. All you have is your word and your actions. That's it." He slips a hand around my waist, pulling me closer and this time I don't push him away. "I promise you, I may seem brash, but I don't take this lightly. I've never proposed marriage to a woman before. I've never really given it a lot of thought except to know that my wife will have to be a *very* exceptional woman."

"Why's that?"

"Because I'm known to drive people mad." He shrugs dismissively.

"Oh really, who would have ever thought that?" I chuckle.

"I know." He jokes, and I step closer.

"Harper."

"Uh huh."

"Can I kiss you?" His finger caresses the side of my face, and my eyes slide closed.

"In the middle of Target?"

"Anywhere, Harper, I'd kiss you anywhere."

Liam's words are like a blinding white light. I can't see anything but him, and I can't look away from the raging need reflecting in his eyes. Then his lips cover mine. Soft kisses at first. Not pecks. Not deep. But enough to feel the warmth from his nearness and the heat from his tongue when I open my mouth to him.

He's probing, stroking, giving, taking. His scent filling my nose, and I taste the citrus sweet tea from lunch. And it's better than I imagined.

Can he feel my heart beating wildly? Can he feel his kiss transforming the dynamic between us? Can I let go long enough to accept that maybe, just maybe Liam is serious about wanting me as much as I'm starting to want…desire…need him?

Liam pulls back resting his forehead on mine. Our breathing in sync, ragged, strained. "Please, Harper."

"What if I'm not who you think I am?" My voice cracks and I pray I'm the woman who makes him happy. Because my foolish heart is falling fast.

"What if I *know* I'll be better, we'll be better, together?"

His emphasis on "know" shimmies from my confused brain and settles in my heart. I feel it warm, throbbing, and it's cementing this complicated, arrogant, protective man to me, and I'm willing to take a chance on us.

"Yes, Liam. Yes, I'll marry you."

CHAPTER 8

LIAM

*H*arper is shaking in my arms. "You won't regret it, sweetheart."

I reach in my pocket and pull out a black velvet box. I drop to one knee.

"Are you serious right now?"

"Harper Price…"

"In the middle of Target, in the baby aisle…"

"I snore, a little," her lopsided smile is killing me, "I leave hair around the sink. I am impatient, I am needy, I am loyal. My mother told me I'd know the moment I found the one. Then I found you." I glance away for the briefest second, I can't stomach the tears in her eyes. "And I know this may be selfish, but I want you forever. Will you marry me?"

I peel open the box. Last night after hours of tossing around, rock hard, wanting Harper, I went to my safe. I dug around and pulled out my mother's ring.

"Liam…" She gasps with tears running down her cheeks.

"It's not big, I can get you another one." I swallow. "It was my mother's."

"I love it." She cups my face, scratching at my beard. "Are you sure, Liam?"

"I'm sure, Harper. But if you take this ring, we are in it together. It's not about anyone but us."

"What do you expect from me as your wife?"

"That you know it's about you and me. I expect honesty, fidelity, friendship, companionship, and that one day you'll come to love me." *Like I love you.* "I'm gruff, but I want a traditional old fashion marriage, minus the quick engagement and vows." I smile. "What about you, what do you expect from me as your husband?"

"The same, but we have to tell my parents when I'm ready. I need time for this all to sink in."

I nod. We'll work out the details. I want to shout for joy but not until we make it official. I pull the ring out slipping the box back in my pocket. "So, Harper, will you do me the honor of being my wife?"

"Yes, Liam, I will."

CHAPTER 9

HARPER

"*I* want you." I inhale deep, the essence of this man crawls inside me. I drove like an insane woman back to the office. The reality of this moment settling in and I surrender to it. I reach for his waistband, kicking the door closed. I pull him to me as my back hits the wall.

"Yes, ma'am."

His nose flairs and his mouth covers mine. His tongue is in my mouth, and I suck it knowing I'm asking for another mistake because Liam is passion and heat and lust and I want everything he has to offer. I've lived a million mistakes. *What's one more?*

"Please, Liam, take me now."

"Baby I apologize our first time shouldn't be in my office," he says between rushed kisses. My neck. My shoulder. Then his hands grip my hips, yanking at the fabric of my dress. I feel the cool air brush my skin as his hands grip my bare ass. He pulls back, lust staring at me. "You don't have on any panties."

I shake my head. For all my proper ways, I prefer no panties, and today I'm glad for it.

"I'm about to show what happens when you bless with me such an amazing gift." Liam snakes down my body, the bottom of my dress is around my waist, he's gripping my ass, and he lifts me to his shoulders without effort. I gasp. I'm no lightweight, and he's kissing the inside of my thighs.

"Liam."

"Shhh…I'm trying to focus." His tongue slips past my folds and dives into my heat. *Gasp*. I whimper from the sweet ecstasy and the precision of his quest. I hold my breath trying to climb up the wall as his tongue assaults me. He holds me tighter, and I grab handfuls of his hair holding on for dear life.

He manages to whisper, "I can't hear you."

"Liam…I can't." I'm panting. Completion is near, and I can't focus with him talking.

"You can and you will." He sucks on my clit. I groan as a heated tickle blazes from my head to my toes. "What did I tell you about expectations?"

"I can't talk…I'm about to…" My hushed whisper is strained. I grip the doorknob with my back pressed into the door for balance. I buck against his face reaching for the release just out of my reach. Then his mouth is gone. My eyes shoot to his. If looks could kill, I'd be dead…a thousand *damn* times. "Liam."

"It's about you and me, Harper. Now, do as I say if you want me." *Lick.* "All of me."

"This is extortion…or blackmail…or something," I argue, trying to pull his face back to me.

"My way, Harper." He nibbles the inside of my thigh, his beard tickling my skin.

"But Glenda?" I'm pleading now. "She'll think I'm some sort of slut. Having sex in the boss' office?"

"I pay the bills. I sign the checks. And I want to finish eating your sweet pussy, Harper. Give me what I want." His eyes hold mine.

"Liam, you can't always have your way." I don't have a leg to stand on, but this man is trying to turn me out, and I love every nanosecond of it.

"Baby, only you would argue with a man begging to please you." He smiles then I see his thick pink tongue. He licks so slow and deep my eyes roll back in my head.

"I'll be mortified, Liam."

"Give me what I want, Harper. We'll both be happy. Let me do this, love." He's teasing my pearl, and my body is revolting against my resistance to give Liam what he wants. "Please."

His tongue plunges in, and I scream relieved to release the pressure building in my chest from holding my breath. His fingers dig into my flesh as he fulfills his promise, devouring me. I'm lost in the stroking, licking, caressing. Blacked out in a zone, I've never felt this way. Never, and I tell him so.

"Then come for me, baby." His mouth is working, and I'm falling. The colors behind my eyes change from black to white. I'm pulling at his beautiful red hair trying to keep from falling. Not on the ground, because his strong shoulders are supporting me. But from falling for him.

The descent is fast and hot, and tension explodes. I squeeze my legs to control the shaking, yelling his name, calling him every deity since the beginning of time.

CHAPTER 10

LIAM

"*T*his is what happens when you let me have my way, Harper." I carry her to my desk pushing all the contents to the floor, I lower her gently making sure her ass is hanging off the edge.

Her kind eyes are now beams of red hot light. I'm holding her up and trying to slip the condom on. She pushes my hands aside and rolls it down. Her eyes leave mine for the briefest second.

"Ready?" I ask.

"Yes."

I wrap an arm around her lower back, and I plunge in. Her wetness holds me like a custom glove as her legs circle my waist. She's taking it. I'm giving it as I inhale the sweet scent of her still on my lips.

Harper is panting. Then she moans, "Liam…"

"Let's do this one together." I lean over bringing her mouth to mine, swallowing her cries. My sweet Harper is a passionate goddess. Our bodies are joined, and I'm fighting my release, I don't want it to end. Not yet.

But I feel her pussy tighten on my cock. "Harper?"

"I want it all."

"Baby, it's yours."

Lost for words, we surrender sucked in by the newness and rawness of our connection. Then her scream collides with my groan as we both surrender.

I gather Harper to my chest carrying her to the couch. And it hits me, this is my fiancée. She'll soon be my wife.

Her head is on my chest, and I'm spent. The sex confirmed my gut reaction to Harper.

"You can't build a marriage on good sex," she whispers, playing with a button on my shirt.

I smile, kissing the top of her head, she still needs convincing. "You can build anything on *great* sex." There's nothing good or mediocre about us. No, together we'll be unstoppable. "The strength of our connection only confirms what we already know sweetheart."

"We don't know each other."

"We have a lifetime for that," I counter.

"Do you propose marriage to all the women gullible enough to have sex with you in your office?"

I place a finger under her chin, lifting her face. The regret staring back at me pisses me off. "Care to repeat that?"

"How many women have you sexed in this office?"

"Harper," I warn.

"What do you do, give Glenda a bonus to slip off and ignore our screams of pleasure?"

"You really on some shit right now."

"Tell me the truth, Liam. I'm a big girl. I can handle it."

I flip her over, pinning her against the couch. Her legs wrap my waist without hesitation. Her brain is fighting us, but her body knows what's up. "Stop fighting us, and trust yourself." I'm pissed at her words.

"Get off me." She pushes against my chest. "I shouldn't have—"

"What let me taste you?" Her eyes cloud in a sexual haze. "You damn right. Because you're mine now, Harper."

She pushes again, and I sit back. I let my words sink in. She jumps up pulling her dress down.

"You really are something else." She squares off her shoulders.

I laugh at the balls on this fine ass woman, still kicking and itching for a fight. "Thank you, Harper."

I see a slight smile on her lips. "For what you incredulous man?"

"I know our marriage will never be boring." I lick my lips for emphasis. I'm not backing down, and neither is she and I feel life pumping through my veins. This is like the ultimate high. "How about round two?"

"Dream on." She spins on her heels. "I'm going to lunch."

"I'll be here since I already *ate*." Harper looks mortified, and I pounce, pinning her body against the door. My hands on either side of her head. "I love you."

"And I think you're insane. You're in lust, yes. Love? I don't believe it." She wiggles under me.

"Tasting your sweet—"

"Liam!"

"I can eat it but I can't—"

"Behave!" I see the hint of laughter in her eyes.

I'm a goner for this woman. It's a done deal. Is the sex part of it? Hell yes! But it's her. One minute she's riding my face, the next she's riding my ass. I'll never have a dull moment with her. And she makes me feel alive. I don't need months or years to tell me Harper is meant for me.

"What if I don't want to behave? I can't behave around you. Not when I know you don't have panties on under that dress. Or I smell the scent of you on my face. Or when I remember how good it felt to be inside you."

She gasps. Our eyes meet. Then I whisper in her ear, "How about I save us the trouble? I'll gas up the plane, fly you to Vegas, and have you back before your lunch break is over."

"What about—"

I pull back searching her eyes for the truth. "Baby don't ever play poker. Your eyes give you away." I caress the side of her face.

"What are they saying now?" Her voice is firm.

I tilt my head. "They say you're scared. You have nothing to be afraid of. Is this fast? Yes. But we'll be just fine."

"I don't know you well enough to believe you." She is staring at my ring on her finger.

"Harper, you believe me. You just don't know it." I tap her chest. "What is your heart saying? And not about your parents or your friends, but your heart, Harper." My heart is pounding in my chest. I'm not used to hearing no and not about something I want.

"That it would be just another heartbreak I'd have to learn to get over." Her eyes meet mine.

"Harper, I wish I had the words to quiet your fears. The words to make you believe that I'd never ever do anything to hurt you. Ask me whatever and I'll answer it. You know I don't want your money. I'll sign a prenup. I'll show you my bank statements to show I can provide for you."

"Why are you insisting on marriage?"

"Because it will make you mine forever."

"You sound like a crazy stalker."

"Harper, I don't have any real family. Glenda is all I have living in this world. And that's not why I want to marry you. I'm asking for marriage because that's where we'll end up anyway." I take a deep breath. "I don't do drugs. I'll keep my vows. I'll give you the wedding of your dreams. I'll make you happy."

I'm feeling like a sucker. But I see her resolve softening again. "I have a beautiful home, you'll love it, and if you don't, we can build another. Huh…" *What are other things women want?* I look in her eyes, and I know what Harper would want, "We can have as many kids as you'd like. I'd like at least four. I am an only child, and it's why I'm alone now. I don't want my children to experience the same." I step back.

"What about your parents?"

"I never met my father. My mother died."

"And you don't have siblings?"

"No."

"What about cousins?"

"Distant ones. But none that I'd consider family." I air quote.

"What about my dad?"

"I don't care about anyone's feelings but yours. I respect your dad, and I'd drive over and talk with him immediately if that's what you want."

"Aren't you the slightest bit concerned about this failing?"

"I trust my gut."

"And your gut is telling you our marriage will last?"

"Yes, Harper." *That and my heart.* I never—never— believed in love at first sight. Not with my financial status and access to what I want, when I want it. But how else can I describe this uncontrollable urge to have her? To take care of her. To love her. And I know Harper is it like I know WEJ will exceed my wildest expectations. Now to convince her, we should do this together.

"That sounds insane, Liam."

"I think you say that because it's expected. You're used to doing what other people expect of you. I don't. Fuck the world. If you live trying to please others, you'll die under the weight of their expectations."

Her eyes dance with wonder. "What's that like?"

"It's freedom, baby."

CHAPTER 11

I *love Harper.* We have six weeks until the roundtable.

Harper and I fight, make love, work, fight, make love, work. The strain of it pulling us apart and wielding us back together. Yet she hasn't told her parents about the engagement. And in the throws of another epic Liam Harper showdown, I removed the ring. It now dangles on the chain near her heart.

"I'll tell them after we close out the roundtable. Promise," she whispers. In my bed is the one place I get all of her. But the haven of my home is like our hiding place. And I'm too damn grown to continue hiding from her *parents*.

"Harper," I lace our fingers, "do you know how hard it is for me to golf with your father and not say anything?" All these years of turning down women and the one woman I want is making my life miserable.

"I'm sorry, but I'm not ready. You said we could do

this at my pace. Now let's get going, we have the final walkthrough at the conference center. I scheduled the caterer to bring the meals plated. And I have a surprise for you."

Harper has taken to planning the way fish take to fresh water. She is thriving and trusting her judgment. The plans exceed my wildest expectations, and we've maxed out on registrations.

The venue is booked. The presenters are set. The people are eager to spend the week with us in Austin. But this doesn't feel the way I hoped.

A few hours later I'm working in my office.

"Knock, knock."

"You're back." I stand and hug Glenda. "Is your place all set?" We sit in the chairs.

"I'm all moved in, and I'll officially call Nashville my home again after the roundtable. Promise me you'll visit me." She reaches for my hand.

"I will. You're not getting rid of me." I squeeze, missing her already.

"Good." She smiles. "Catch me up."

"We're set. We finalized everything this morning and Harper received confirmation from the mayor's office."

"What?"

"Yeah, she called some people, and he'll be the keynote speaker on Friday night."

"How does this feel? You've been killing us all to make it happen."

I smile. "It feels surreal."

"But…"

"I think Harper will back out of our engagement."

"Why?" She turns in her chair.

"I just know."

"How do you feel about it?"

"Rejection of the worst kind." My voice trails off. I can talk to Glenda about anything. This is where my walls don't exist, and I'm preparing myself for the worst.

"Don't over think this, Liam, and don't push her. Because if you push, Harper will push back. Give her time."

"Give her time…give her time…it's been five months and I haven't met any of her family. How would you feel about that?" Harper is arousing old fears and insecurities.

"Liam, don't shut her out."

I can't look at Glenda because she'll see it in my eyes. Not knowing is worse than her initial rejection. Over the months she's eased into our relationship, but I know we're no further along now than we were then.

"I need to get ready for a few calls."

"Okay. Call me if you need me." Glenda kisses the top of my head, hugging me to her chest. "It will all work out."

I watch her leave my office. It's time I admit it to Harper and myself that maybe she's right, perhaps this won't work. Better now than waiting only to watch another person leave.

Then I do what I do best…work.

I'm sitting outside WEJ parked next to Liam's car. The roundtable was a success and yet I feel like we're worse than ever. I dial his number, and it goes straight to voicemail.

"Babe, I'm watching the twins tonight. Call me or stop by and keep me company." *Love you.*

I rush across town to relieve Charlee. Hunter and Ben left on an after babymoon. The guys and I are helping her parents keep the kids until they return. Tonight's my night.

"Yay! Auntie Harp is here." Charlee is wiggling BJs arms in the air. Then she chews on his jaws and his round belly. His precious giggles make me laugh.

"Where's HJ?" I take BJ from her sniffing his baby scented skin. "Hey, precious baby."

"HJ is sleep. Thank god! Watching twins is the best birth control."

"I bet." She fills me in on the last feeding, diaper changes, and she's headed towards the door.

"So, when's the big day?"

I stop bouncing BJ on my hip. "The roundtable was last week."

"I didn't forget about that, I'm talking about your wedding announcement. Did I miss it?" Charlee's been jet setting with her new man.

"No." I start bouncing again, turning my back to her.

"And why not?" She steps around me bringing us nose to nose.

"Because we haven't." I nibble on BJ's chubby cheeks to keep from making eye contact with Charlee. I've been waiting for the change to happen. For Liam to turn from my handsome Irish prince to the frog, I'm used to. But he hasn't.

"That man was ready to marry you six months ago. What do you believe he's thinking now?"

"He's cool. We're cool." I reason. "Why mess up a good thing when we're happy?"

We still clash like titans but in a manner that makes me feel truly alive. I can't imagine not having Liam in my life.

"Are you sure about that, Harper? Liam doesn't strike me as the most patient man."

"We're good. Now go, you're barging in on my alone time with my Little Man."

"All right girl. Love you."

"Love you too." I close the door with Liam on my mind. I call him. No answer.

I'll head straight to his place once Parker arrives to relieve me.

~

I'm haunted by Charlee's words as I arrive at Liam's house. He wasn't lying about his home, the five bedrooms, two-story house is enormous, fit for a family. He had it professionally decorated down to the formal dining room.

I take the stairs two at a time. I burst into his room, and my man is asleep. I toss my clothes aside crawling into bed with him.

"Hey, baby," he mumbles kissing me. He grips my hips pulling my body against his. "How are the boys?"

"Perfect." I smile. "Hey babe, are you happy?"

Liam stops stirring turning me to face him. "What's going on?" He rubs his eyes.

"I'm just curious is all." I scratch at his beard, loving the feel of it.

"I'm happy with you, but not our circumstances."

"What does that mean?"

"What I said," he says with heavy sarcasm. "When am I meeting your parents, as your man? Your fiancé?"

"Soon."

"When Harper?" His eyes drill into me.

"I'm not ready yet."

"I'm not ready, I'm not ready. I agreed to give you time, but time doesn't mean forever." He rolls over tossing the covers back. "I'm starting to believe you have no intention of marrying me."

"Why would you say that?" My tone matches his.

"Harper, stop shittin' me. You don't want to be here, fine. Keep coming here every night to fuck me and living a happy-go-lucky life with your parents during the day. Like this relationship is a fucking joke." He stomps off, slamming the door to the bathroom.

The echo slams through my body.

"Liam, you don't say that and walk off." I scramble to my feet.

"Says who, Harper Anne?" He opens the door, his ripped body on display. Damn if I don't want him right now. "And don't stand there looking at my dick."

"I'm sorry, Liam. I'll tell them. I promise." He's right. But what if I tell them and it ruins everything? And what if this life I'm building with him doesn't last? Then what? I shake my head, Liam won't let that happen. I won't let that happen. "I'll ask them to dinner and tell them. Okay?"

"Yeah, whatever."

Liam heads to the bathroom, and I'm left standing alone. I hear the shower and follow the sound. His hand is braced on the wall as the water falls down his back. I open the glass door and step inside.

"Baby, I'm sorry. I'm just scared."

"Scared of what, Harper. I love you. I love you with every fucking fiber of my being. But that's not enough for you." The bridled anger in his tone is killing me. "You care more about what other people think, and I don't live my life like that. I don't live my life like *this*."

I place my hands on his back, rubbing in circles. I grab the soap lathering it up. He's right. I cover his back with kisses. I can't lose him.

"I love you," I whisper.

"Do you Harper? Because you have a fucked up way of showing it."

CHAPTER 13

We're laying back to back. Not just his words but the tone is bouncing around in my mind. I toss and turn. I have to fix this. I really love Liam. He's been everything he said he'd be and I have to face my parents. Tell them that I love him and I want to be his wife. Knowing that I've somehow messed this up is breaking my heart.

I roll over.

"Where are you going, Harper?"

"Home."

Liam falls back. I see the uncertainty in his eyes, and I put it there.

"Come here, baby." I snuggle in his arms, laying my head on his chest. "I know I rushed you. I couldn't help myself. Now's the time to level with me."

"I want—"

"Don't, Harper. Don't just blurt some shit out. Is this where you want to be? By my side, in my bed, in my home as my wife. It's plain and simple. I'm not going to be a little secret that you and your friends giggle about. I want to mean more to you than that."

"I'll take care of it, and we can set a date."

I climb on top of Liam kissing my way across his chest. This part of our relationship comes with ease. The giving and taking without expectations. Truth be told I'm tired of the secrets too. But telling my parents will make my fairytale real.

Liam cups my face in his hands. "Babe, we can handle whatever happens together. You believe me don't you?"

"Yes, Liam." I kiss the inside of his wrist and stare into his eyes. "Make love to me."

"Harper…"

"Please…" I kiss him, and I try to convey all the love I have in my body, my being for him. "You're not in this alone." My lips touch his neck, his chest, I lick the peak of his nipples. I use my tongue to trace the valleys of his abs until my nose teases the hairs around his manhood.

"Harper…"

Letting him feel my tongue as his hands grab the back of my neck. He's growing harder the more I swirl my tongue around the head. Then I take him in my mouth. The power I feel over this strong man is unmatched by the responsibility I feel for his pleasure. Pleasure he's given me over and over. Love he's given me so freely. I've been selfish and scared, and I'm not anymore.

His body bucks under me, and I'm ready to ride. I climb his body, he kisses me rough and hard, and I position myself over him.

"Are you sure?" he asks, rubbing at my entrance without entering.

"I trust you."

Liam pushes inside me, filling me completely. Skin to skin. His growls vibrate through my body and off the walls. We move together, I follow his tempo rolling my hips to increase the friction between our bodies. His presses harder and harder. His steady gaze jolts my heart. *I love this man.*

Our mouths crash into each other as we ride through the throes of love. I beg for more, and he obligates. His whispers of I love you...you're mine...until we spill over.

"I was scared." I kiss his chest, afraid to look in his eyes.

"Of what, Harper, I love you more than—" I cover his mouth with my hand and he kisses my fingertips.

"I know. I know, Liam, and you were right. But I didn't want to jinx it, to ruin a *great* thing."

He flips me over. "Harper, nothing can make me stop loving you." The sincerity in his eyes causes tears to fill my eyes.

"How do you know?"

"My parents met and married fast. My mother said it was love at first sight. She told me I'd find you." I see his smile shining in the dark. "I've never felt this way about anyone else. And I don't want to, Harper."

"I don't deserve you."

"We deserve each other. You make me better."

I'm a sloppy mess. "I love you, Liam."

"You'll get all this and more. Fix this, baby, and become my wife. I'll show you, this is just the beginning."

His words erase the lingering doubts. Maybe nice doesn't finish last because I feel first in his book. I'm about to make my man the happiest man in the world.

CHAPTER 14

HARPER

he waitress shows me to my parents' table. Liam and I stayed in until he had to leave for dinner with Glenda and I agreed to meet with my parents. Liam wanted to join us, but I want to tell them alone in a public place. I don't think they'll freak out, but telling them I'm engaged may shock them a *little*.

"Hey, Honey." My mother stands, and I kiss her cheek. She's as petite as my father is big. My daddy the big Texas cowboy.

"Dad." I squeeze his shoulders in a hug, kissing his cheek too.

I sit across from them ordering a glass of wine. They update me on the recent round of visits to our ranches. We have five with cattle, chickens, and horses. I used to make the rounds with them until I started working with Platinum Prestige and even less since I've taken over Glenda's old job at WEJ.

"I asked to join you guys because I have something to tell you."

"What is it, Honey?" Mom grabs my hand, and I swallow down the last of my wine.

"I'm—"

"Harper? Mrs. and Mr. Price?" I turn to see Marcel.

"Pull up a chair, Son," Dad offers.

"Don't mind if I do." *The bullfrog is back.*

"Actually I'd like to have this conversation with you guys alone," I insist.

"Oh, Harper, stop being a brat," Marcel jokes with a greedy look on his beady face. He sits in the empty chair next to me. My folks ask about his parents and his work at the law firm. How did I think for a moment about tying myself to this guy? I must have been deaf, dumb, and delirious.

"Yeah, I recently made partner."

"Congrats, Son. Glad to hear it. You about ready to turn this thing into something serious?" Dad glances between us. He always liked Marcel, but I love Liam.

"Dad, Mom—"

"I'm trying, Sir," he cuts me off, and I kick him under the table.

"Mom, Dad, I'm engaged." I blurt it out.

"When?" Dad's face hits the floor.

"To Marcel?" Mom's eyes go straight to my ringless left hand.

"No, to me."

CHAPTER 15

I saw Harper the moment she entered the restaurant. What are the chances we'd select the same spot? Glenda saw her too. My hope dwindling by the second.

"What are you thinking, Liam?"

"I'm about to cut that dude's arm off." I see the tension in Harper's posture from here.

"That sounds pleasant."

I cut my eyes towards her. "She's supposed to tell her parents about our engagement tonight, and now she's with him." *Picture perfect.* A picture I obviously don't fit in or else I'd be over there and not here.

"You don't know that. All we can see is the back of her head."

"And his arm on the back of her chair. Let's get out of here."

"Liam, you can't leave like this."

"Glenda, I took your advice, and it's an epic fail. I'm in

love with a woman who's either with some other dude or too scared to tell her parents about me."

"Or she just needs time. You're always a hot head. Chill out. Trust her."

"How much time? I'm giving her all I have, and if it's not enough, I need to move on. Let's go."

Glenda stands, I don't let the disappointment in her eyes deter me. I told Harper where I stand, what I expect, and I'm not down for the fuckin' heartbreak. I toss a tip on the table.

I grip the back of Glenda's chair to help her up. She stands in front of me placing a hand on my chest. "For me, Liam, go over there. Not as a hot head, but as a friend, as the man who loves her. Please."

I glance over at the table and see the dude's hand on Harper's shoulder. I shake my head. "Nah, I'm good."

"You're better with Harper. I haven't seen you this happy since you lost your mother. It breaks my heart to see you hurting like this. So, don't be a chicken shit."

"A what?" I laugh despite my heart crumbling. "A chicken shit. Really, Glenda?"

"I have to get your attention. Go." She pushes me in the direction of the table.

I take a deep breath. This is for the best. If she plans to leave me and move on, at least I'd know the truth, I tell myself, but it makes the ache worse. Harper does make me better. My gut was absolutely right about her, about us. And now she's about to ruin it.

I stand behind her and hear, "Mom, Dad, I'm engaged."

I step forward, and the coward has sense enough to remove his arm from behind my woman. Harper stands and grabs my hand.

"Liam and I are engaged," she says smiling. I search her eyes, this is the feisty Harper I know and love.

"Liam, care to explain?" James asks.

"Harper and I met, and we've been seeing each other for six months."

"Six months!" the three sing.

"Yes, Mom and Dad," she rolls her eyes at the loser, "six months. I didn't tell you, but life finally gave me what I needed and wanted." I see the love in her eyes. I squeeze her hand in support. "I was scared to tell you after having so many duds." She turned to the jerk still lingering. "You can leave now."

We sit at the table together then I remember Glenda. I wave her over.

Harper continues, "We plan to get married in Vegas. Want to join us?"

My breath catches, and I grab her face kissing her senseless. I hear the collective gasp, but I tongue my woman down.

"I'm sorry, Liam. Can you please gas up the plane? I have a man to marry."

Glenda is crying, her parents are in shock, and my woman looks happy. "Are you sure?"

"You said it's you and me, right? Well, I'm ready for you and me to become us. Are you coming, Mom and Dad?"

EPILOGUE

LIAM

"*A*dmit it, I'm right," I demand laying butt naked with my wife flying over the Atlantic. We sent her parents and her guys home to Austin and Glenda to Nashville.

"I will not. Your head will swell to the size of a watermelon. And I happen to like your *head* the way it is." She winks.

We're en route to Paris for our honeymoon.

"Fine don't admit that I was right about us getting married. But you can admit I was right about you working for WEJ."

"I'll give you that." She crawls on top of me. I run my hands over the swell of her hips cupping her ass. "That's only because you've agreed to share me with Platinum Prestige. But now it's time for you to pay up."

"Have I told you how much I love your ass?"

"Yes," she kisses my chest, "you have, but I'll never tire of hearing it."

I slide inside Harper. My world is complete with her in it. She's bucking with each stroke, a sight I'll *never* tire of.

"You owe me three wishes."

"Name 'em."

"A year jet lease for Platinum Prestige," she squeezes out between moans.

"Done."

"I want my own office at WEJ."

I grunt near completion. "Done."

Her body jerks and pleasure overtakes us. Harper falls relaxed in my arms, and I brush the sweat from her forehead. Her eyes are heavy, fighting to remain open.

How did I get so lucky?

"That's only two, love."

"I already got number three." She smiles snuggling beneath the blanket I use to cover us.

"And what is that?"

Harper opens her eyes. "You, Liam Walsh, I wished for you. My very own Mr. Right. My very own Prince Charming. I spent so much time kissing frogs I thought I'd never find the perfection of what I have with you."

My eyes get a little misty. I kiss her with all the love I feel inside, as her moans vibrate through my body. "You trying to get pregnant on this plane? And you know I always get what I want."

"Damn right, with your arrogant ass," Harper teases.

"And you love it."

"You know I do."

Her laughter fills the plane and my heart. I flip her

wrapping her legs around my waist, ready to love her across the ocean and back.

"The world is ours. I'm looking forward to our forever together, Mrs. Walsh. Do you believe me, baby?"

A sweet smile crosses her face. "Yes, Liam, now stop talking and make love to me. The world can wait until *after* our honeymoon."

AUTHOR'S NOTE

I said YES to a holiday romance writing project in 2019.

Ten authors. Ten holidays. Ten steamy romances. And we've all said yes to taking this journey together.

My ten stories are novella length. I think they're great for an evening of reading with your favorite glass of wine or tea. :) And I had the group of guys to make this series happen.

Then struts in Hunter and her squad, her guys. They came to me years ago. I love a good millionaire or billionaire romance like the next woman. But a few of my readers emailed me asking about a female millionaire. I thought why settle for one if I can write ten. **insert evil laugh**

I hope you enjoyed book one with Harper and Liam. Will you join me for the rest of the year as they build Platinum Prestige—one fly millionaire woman and hot guy at a time?

Don't miss a single release. Join my newsletter at

http://www.janesedixon.com/subscribe to get updates and reader specials FIRST.

In closing, please leave a review. It helps others find my work and it keeps the lights on, if you know what I mean. ;)

I'll "see" you all soon.

Happy Reading,
Ja'Nese Dixon
www.janesedixon.com

P.S. Again, there are more Steamy Sensations Holiday Love stories available now. See them all on my website: http://www.janesedixon.com/steamy-sensations.

LEAVE A REVIEW

Did you enjoy *Privileged Love*?

Please leave a book review **HERE**. Reviews are extremely important and it helps me continue sharing my books with fellow readers.

JOIN MY NEWSLETTER

Be the FIRST to know!

Consider joining my newsletter? http://www.janesedixon.com/subscribe Be the first to know about releases and specials. You can unsubscribe anytime.

It's Valentine's Day.

I run to my favorite bar determined to figure out how I managed to lose my man and my inheritance in one night. The man is replaceable, but my monthly stipend is not.

I'm Hunter Preston. My friends call me Jo and I'm the only child to a media mogul. I was traveling the world, living my best life, until Daddy dropped a million-dollar bomb, annihilating my boujee world.

Double or nothing.

He gave me thirty days to pitch a million dollar business concept, or I can say goodbye to my trust fund.

So, here I am with my girls, trying to get more than selfie advice, when Ben, the sexy bartender—who either abhors me or he's immune to my flirting—offers to help write the business plan under one condition. He wants $50,000.

$50k to get $1 mil sounds reasonable until I remember how hot he is and how off-limits he is and how he wants nothing to do with a woman like me.

I'm screwed, pass me another drink.

COMING SOON ~ BLAZIN' LOVE
SERIES

BOOK 3: EXCLUSIVE LOVE

**This might be my chocolate covered
second chance at love.**

It's Easter Sunday.

I'm sitting on the pew next to my Mom, handling
my daughter duties when HE—Darius Grant— walks in

sparking thoughts that guarantee I'm going straight to hell with gasoline panties on.

I'm Charlee Stuart. I've joined my best friends in starting an elite concierge service. My assignment is to find premium services for our upscale clientele. Truth is, I have no idea what I'm doing, but I won't fail my guys.

He takes the seat in front of me blocking my view. At six foot, fine, and filthy rich, I'm hoping I won't be struck by lightning. Then I remember Darius is off limits. But his chocolates may be just what I need to test my skills of persuasion.

I'm not the kind of woman to chase a dude, but I might hop in his direction. And I'm making a promise on this hard-ass pew before the Man and my momma, that I will not…will not fall for Darius again.

Then he turns and winks in my direction. For the love of things hot and tempting, please...

Father...take me now!

Coming April 2019!

Get the Alert!

Millions of adoring fans dream of having one night with him, but only she has access to his heart.

Born with three commas in his bank account and melodies in his veins, Marques Carter is the rising prince of R&B. But not even his family name can guarantees success.

Brione Allen is a smart woman that made a dumb decision: trusting the wrong man. He blackmailed her family and now she's bound by a debt they knew she couldn't pay.

A chance meeting at his concert leads to an encrypted proposal: One week, one hundred thousand dollars, one incriminating secret. But when extortion and family ties expose them to the worst of the limelight, which secrets will they keep…and which will threaten their small light of hope?

Get Your Copy on Amazon
or Read in Kindle Unlimited!

CHAPTER 1

The same time every week for three years and the call got no easier. Brione Allen sat on the couch and blew out a deep breath. Dial the number. Ask for Kayla. But the knot in her stomach told the utter truth. Nothing about this was easy for her.

She tapped the numbers by memory, adding it to her favorites was something she couldn't stomach, not after all they'd done to her.

"Hello."

"Good evening Mrs. Bradley is Kayla around?" She stopped asking to speak with her hoping to gain a sense of control in the situation, but they held her captive with a vice grip on her heart.

"Hello to you too Brione." Her dusty voice held an air of censorship. "I'll call for her."

Kayla had a nanny, private school, and just about everything a little girl could want.

"Brione." She cringed at hearing his voice.

"Stewart, I was holding for Kayla."

"She'll have to call you back."

"But today is my—"

"Talk to you later."

The line disconnected and Brione screamed. No one heard her, and no one cared. Alone in her fancy plush prison, she'd gladly trade for their freedom.

She fell back on the couch and stared at the ceiling fan and her cellphone rang. She popped up anticipating the sweet sound of Kayla's voice. But the screen displayed another welcomed caller.

"Eliana Marshall. To what do I owe this honor?" Laughter flowed through the phone, Eliana was the only person she let close. The only person she trusted. The only person who knew the truth.

"Let's see...I'm your best friend. So I need no reason to call other than to hear your wonderful voice." Brione smiled. "Second, I'm flying into town, and I refuse any excuse you make for not seeing me."

Brione gripped the phone to her ear as she toyed with the hem of her blouse. She'd rushed home from work for nothing.

"I apologized a million times. But you plan to milk it dry," she joked pulling her stocking covered feet beneath her body and relaxed.

"I plan to milk it until it turns to powder if that will get your butt out of that condo. I will *not* take no for an answer."

"Milk it dry *and* add in a level of guilt to the recipe."

"You got it." They laughed. "How are you?"

"I've been better." Brione looked around the room, furnished with the finest, reeking of their wealth. "You're heading here for the weekend?"

"No, I'm heading back indefinitely. Bruce and his wife are expecting twins, and they're keeping a close watch on her. We're planning to hang out in Houston until the babies arrive. Her doctor and family are all there. So, it could be a couple of months or longer."

"Yay!" Brione sat up, excited. "It will be nice to have you in town for a while."

"Just know I plan to pop up on your doorstep and drag you to a party or two while I'm there." Brione shook her head knowing they would have a battle ahead.

"How are you enjoying your job?"

Brione listened as Eliana shared her love of working for Bruce Daniels. She bounced around from Atlanta to Houston and back as his assistant.

"I can't believe the luck I've had with getting this job. It is stressful but fun. I'll be assisting Marques for a while too."

"Who is that?" The name sounded familiar, in a fuzzy, vague way.

"What rock do you live under?"

"The law school rock." She snickered. "I don't have time for anything but class and studying. Well, that and my side gig."

"Side gig?"

"Eliana, who is Marques?"

"Oh, yeah. How do you *not* know who he is?" Her amazement was evident by the squeak in her voice.

"He's a caramel dipped...tall, muscled...*god* in living color."

Brione lifted a brow at Eliana's description. "All that?"

"Yes, he's the epitome of sexy. Too bad he's my boss." She let out a sigh. "Anyway, he's an R&B singer from Atlanta. I guess you wouldn't know him since he's more underground." She was all business. "He is the flagship artist of Rockstar Entertainment. We're preparing to release an EP then his debut album."

Brione tried to picture this caramel sexy god. Her failed attempt morphed into her last dalliance that turned her life upside down, inside out, and left Brione estranged from her family.

"That sounds like a lot of work." Brione didn't listen to the radio and rarely watched TV. Her sights were set on securing an associate's position with a major law firm. Fun took a backseat.

"It is, which is part of the reason for my call." Eliana said.

"Oh, it wasn't just to hear my wonderful voice?"

"Of course."

"Yeah, yeah, yeah. Spill it, Honey." Brione walked to the kitchen and opened the freezer, pushing around the contents until she found the frozen lasagna.

"Do you still help with events?"

"Yes, what's up?" She peeled back the corner of the lid and popped the plastic bowl into the microwave. Then she leaned a hip against the counter.

"Bruce's anticipated maternity leave and Marques' EP

has opened a lot of doors for me. They've asked me to oversee the launch with hopes of promoting me to A&R."

"Congrats!"

"Thanks, but hold it for now. I still need to get through this project."

"So, basically it's an interview."

"Exactly."

"How can I help?" Brione dropped her head and chuckled at the faint sounds of Eliana's clapping. Eliana could make it happen without her, but Brione wanted to see her friend succeed. "I didn't say yes yet."

"But you will." Eliana blew a kiss through the phone. "I want to host a release party in Houston, and I'd love to bring you in. It pays good, and I'm almost certain I can get you the gig."

"Really? But I've never done a music event."

"Don't worry about that. Your work is impeccable, you're organized, timely, and you work well under extreme pressure. Are you free Saturday?"

"Yes, how about ten?"

"That's perfect. Get together your portfolio and let's meet at the cafe on Saturday. I'll try to get either Bruce or Marques there too. That way I can cross two tasks off my list at once."

"I like the sound of that."

"You would, Miss Planner Chic. I maintain, where you thrive. One day, I'll grow up to be just like you."

Brione shook her head as if Eliana could see her. "No, ma'am. Grow up to be like you, and you'll be just fine."

"The thought of peanut butter and honey back in business is enticing don't you think."

"Houston ain't ready for us," Brione added.

Eliana's robust laughter rang through the phone. "Girl, if only they knew! And for totally selfish reasons, it would be a lifesaver to have your help *and* get to spend time with you without you skipping out on me."

They haven't seen each other in years, for one reason or another. But Brione missed her too. "I got you. When we're done, they're going to beg you to take that position. And I'll be there at 9:45 ready to rock n' roll."

"Awesome. I'll text you if anything changes. I gotta go, we're about to land." Eliana said.

"Be safe." The microwave beeped.

"I will. Love you Peanut Butter." Eliana giggled.

"Love you too Honey." They disconnected, Brione stood staring at the phone for a minute considering their long friendship.

Eliana was her roommate in college, their running nicknames came when all they could afford was Ramen noodles, and peanut butter and jelly, except Eliana, liked hers with honey or syrup.

Music was Eliana's passion like organizing events was Brione's. However, she knew her love of centerpieces and tulle could not lead to her desired destination.

Brione gathered her hot food from the microwave and walked to the dining room, she turned into an office. She stared at the stack of textbooks. She entered law school for two reasons: money and time. The family connections between the Bradleys and her parents guaranteed her seat. But her high GPA landed her a full ride.

She cleared a space for her bowl, tonight she'd study and tomorrow she'd order pizza and work on her portfolio. She lowered into the chair in front of her laptop, placing her food aside. She opened the oversized law book and turned to the cases she needed to read and analyze for class tomorrow.

She leaned over the keyboard and forked a chunk of lasagna, she cradled her hand beneath it to keep the sauce from dripping onto her expensive textbooks. She popped it into her mouth and did a chair dance as the ricotta cheese and Italian sausage made her taste buds happy, momentarily overlooking that it almost burnt her tongue. She pushed the bowl back to let it cool and read the first legal case when her phone rang again. The little face on the screen made her heart race with joy.

"Hello, Sweet Pea." Her voice trembled, she took a deep breath.

"Hi!" Brione could envision her chubby cheeks, full eye lashes, and radiant smile.

"I think this is the best surprise I've had all day." Her giggle warmed Brione's heart. "How was school today?"

Kayla talked about crayons and finger painting. Her new best friend and a boy pulling her pigtails. All the things Brione had to experience by phone and not in person. And as soon as the call started it ended, sending exaggerated kisses through the phone to the tune of Kayla's sweet laughter with promises of talking with her again on Saturday.

Life wasn't fair. That was too tall of an order.

Brione used the fork to cut into the cooler lasagna. She had stopped crying about it and questioning why long ago, instead she dealt with it, taking blow by blow and somehow managing to bounce back. But tonight she wanted to sit in it. From the sting of the scheduled phone calls to Stewart consistently dangling their freedom like cheese enticing a rat, reminding herself that she had a plan. This ache in her chest was only temporary.

One day she and Kayla would live under the same roof. Holding on to this goal kept her in one piece.

Kayla motivated Brione to work hard and she vowed not to repeat the same mistake twice. Men like the dreamy caramel sex god Eliana drooled over were bad news. Stewart was one of them. He walked into a room and every woman—married, single, it didn't matter—wanted him. She'd thought herself lucky.

Brione snickered at her foolish youth. None of them cared about what she wanted in life. Her goals. Her desires. To the Bradleys, her parents, Stewart, she was their pawn, their minion, their tool. *So they thought.*

She couldn't afford to crack. She ate the rest of her dinner, deciding to study first then get her portfolio together for her meeting with Eliana.

To get Kayla back, she needed money and landing the job with Eliana to organize Marques' event could be the break she'd prayed for.

*W*alking into Coffee Confessions had a ring of a homecoming for Marques Carter. He had spent many days hanging around waiting on Bruce to finish a shift before they went to the studio. Houston saved him and got his life back on course. Now that he was back, he hoped lightning would strike again for them.

He pulled the baseball cap lower to disguise himself. The release of his first official video last week gave him more than his usual double takes. In Atlanta, he couldn't go anywhere without people recognizing him, here offered a reprieve. But he didn't want to take any chances, welcoming the way people bumped right past him. It added another reason he loved being back in Houston.

Marques arrived early to meet with Bruce. He scanned the room, spotting a few empty tables and made his way to the line. He lifted his head to read the menu when he felt a soft bump behind him. He turned around and had to glance down at a petite woman.

"Excuse me." She held up a hand then reached out to stabilize a mug rocking back and forth on the shelf. "I was trying to miss the stroller and then the display and…" Her voice stalled as she finally looked up at him. Her lips parted in surprise. "Huh, sorry."

He chuckled. "I think I'll live."

She nodded without speaking as their gazes held. Marques let his eyes survey her light brown skin paired with jet black hair. It was curled softly brushing the sides of her face in a chic bob. Her heart-shaped face and doe eyes held curiosity as her full lashes brushed her high cheekbones with each exaggerated blink behind black frames. But when he zeroed in on her full lips coated with a hint of gloss, her tongue darted out and a groan reached his ears. He didn't know if it came from him or her.

"Andrew Carter." Using his legal name seemed appropriate as he extended a hand ready to see if her skin was as soft as it appeared.

"Brione Allen." Her smooth husky tone reminded him of a midnight radio jockey. The type of voice that held intrigue, mystery, and allure.

She accepted his hand and lightning passed from her touch through his body. *Damn*. Her eyes flashed to meet his as his heart rate tripled. He studied her thoughtfully, appreciating the heat lingering in the depths of her brown eyes.

"Welcome to Coffee Confessions, give in to your

guilty pleasure. How can I be of service?" The barista behind the counter asked and Marques was at a loss for words. He still held her delicate hand in his thinking Miss Brione Allen was a guilty pleasure he'd gladly give in to. But judging by the penetrating stare she gave him as she snatched her hand away from his, he doubted she was on the menu.

"I'm sorry, I need a moment to review the menu. Brione after you." He extended his hand towards the counter and she stepped forward. She appeared as surprised as he was. The chemistry between them was as real as the nose on his face.

"Huh, sure." She stepped to the counter and tossed her purse on her shoulder like a barrier between them. *No, baby girl, that purse ain't gonna save you.*

She started to order and the sounds of the room faded into oblivion as Marques scanned the length of her body, the curve of her backside, and...

"And for you sir?" The barista wiggled his eyebrows. Heat rose to Marques' face, *caught*. But her hips were too tempting to ignore in pants that left no curve to the imagination.

"Our order is not tog—"

"Make it two of what she's having." He passed his credit card and turned back to Brione.

"That's not necessary."

"You're welcome," he teased, her expression much too severe for him.

Her eyes softened, "Thank you."

Brione stepped to the side and waited as Marques

collected his receipt. They stood in heated silence both snagging discreet glances at the other waiting for their coffee. He had no clue what she ordered, thankfully he wasn't allergic to anything.

His senses were ablaze with her nearness. The closest comparison would be the moment he completed a new song. It gave the dueling emotions of exhilaration and exhaustion simultaneously.

"Are you off to work today?" He noticed the button up blouse and dress slacks.

"No, I'm meeting a friend. And you?"

"Business." She scanned his body in a sweeping motion. He wore a baseball cap with jeans and shirt. His goal was to blend in with the good people of Houston. He wished now that he'd given it more thought. Her mouth took on an unpleasant twist. "What you don't approve of my casual attire?"

"Oh no. I think it must be nice."

He searched her eyes and wished he could read her mind. The barista called his name for the order. Marques passed a cup to her and grabbed his own. The place was filling up quickly. He snagged a table and pulled out a chair for her.

"Join me while you wait." She hesitated. "Please." Brione slowly lowered to the chair. The floral scent of her perfume couldn't compete with the aroma of the coffee beans but it was a soft statement of her presence in the busy cafe.

Marques sat across from her finding it hard to contain the odd sensation in the pit of his stomach. He took a drink of the hot coffee to distract himself. The taste of caramel and whipped cream warmed his mouth. "This is delicious. What is it?"

"A custom drink. It's my favorite." She lifted the cup to her mouth and took a sip too. Remnants of her gloss left on the white lid.

"I'll have to get this again." He grabbed his phone and snapped a picture of the sleeve. "So Brione tell me, are you from Houston?"

She sat her cup on the table, pulling closer. Their knees brushed, her eyes widened. "No."

He waited for her to continue, she crossed her hands over the table. "Are you always this talkative?"

Her husky laughter rippled through the air. "No, it takes me a minute to warm up to people."

He nodded. Brione dropped her hands to her lap, "What about you? Are you from here?"

"No, I'm from Georgia."

"You said you're here on business. What type of business are you in?"

"I'm in a family business. I'm taking a little time off before we enter a busy season." It was obvious she didn't recognize him. It made him relax, he didn't feel "on."

"Do you travel often?" She asked.

"Not as often as I'd like."

"So you enjoy traveling?"

He nodded, "I do. It is a love of mine, I acquired it as a child. I traveled a lot with my parents." He took a drink of his coffee. He joined his father on many tours over the years. "The food, architecture, music, museums, I love all of it."

"Where all have you visited?" The warmth of her smile echoed in her voice.

He crossed his arms over his chest and extended his legs. "I visited, at last count, 40 or so of the great states of America. I've hit the tourist spots. Australia, Canada, South Africa, Rome, London, Egypt, I love it there too. Dubai, New Zealand, India, China, Morocco, Italy, Bali. There are more but you put me on the spot."

"Tell me about your favorite place." She leaned over the table and rested her chin in her hand. Her eyes bright and inquisitive.

"Uh…" her smile made it hard to think straight, he searched his mind, "I can't pick just one. My most recent trip was to Bora Bora."

"That place is on my wish list." A smile danced on her lips, heat coursed through his veins. *Get a grip!*

"Put a star by it. It is a place you'll never forget. The warmth of the water. Its vibrant turquoise color. There's something magical and healing about the island."

Her expression stilled and grew serious.

"Add this one to your wish list too." He wanted to see her smile again. "Torres del Paine National Park."

The spark returned. "Where is that?"

Marques leaned forward enjoying the light in her eyes. "It's in Chile. There's more sheep than people but the valleys are the most vibrant green and the sky the bluest blue you'll ever see. There is a small window when the weather is appropriate but it is worth it." He winked and something told him she mentally noted every word.

He wondered what she was thinking as she dropped her head, brushing her hair behind her ears. Her phone buzzed against the table and Brione glanced down at the screen.

"That's my friend." She held up her phone and finished her coffee. "We have to reschedule."

She stood from the table and leaned over to toss the empty cup in the trash.

"Would you like another?"

"No, I have studying to do."

"Studying?" He hoped to prolong her departure.

"I'm a law student." The glimmer in her eyes dulled.

"If I remember correctly there are three of them here."

"You are absolutely correct." She placed her purse on her shoulder and picked up a black portfolio. He missed that earlier.

"Would you like to grab lunch or something?"

"I really need to go." She shook her head and glanced at her phone. "Thank you for the coffee and the conversation." An easy smiled played at the corners of her mouth.

"No, thank you for this wonderful concoction." He held up the cup shaking it.

"You're welcome. Have a nice day." She turned to leave and he reached for her arm.

"Take my number. I'm in town for a couple weeks. I *really* would like to see you again."

"I don't have time. I—"

"Take it...just in case. Pass me your phone and I'll enter it."

She searched his eyes for so long he thought she'd say no again.

"Okay." She hesitantly passed her unlocked phone, holding the top with the tip of her fingers, as if trying to avoid his touch.

He entered his personal cellphone number and placed the phone in her open palm. "I'll talk with you soon."

*B*rione sat to study for finals, she had two weeks left before summer break. But his voice, his smile barraged her. "Study Bri!"

Thoughts of coffee with Andrew had her head in the clouds. The way his head fell back when he laughed. The twinkle in his eyes when he teased her. It was a chasm in time that passed too fast, she wanted more.

Closing her eyes she estimated his height was close to six feet, the outlines of his shoulders strained against the fabric of his shirt. He stood before her with his hands shoved in his pockets and a killer smile wide with perfect white teeth. His classically handsome features made him beautiful for a man.

People passed their table slowing to gawk at him, not once did he look away or acknowledge their presence. She wondered what his hair looked like beneath the cap but figured it really didn't matter. The man could be bald and she was sure she'd find him absolutely breathtaking —star quality.

Brione shook her head trying to rattle the images of him from her memories. But it proved impossible.

She tried reading the case at least ten times with no luck. But his soft encouragement, add this one to your wish list, rendered it impossible. Adding him to her list sound better. *Forget it.*

She opened her laptop and clicked on an internet browser. She typed in, Torres del Paine National Park and pressed enter. The results populated, her inner child didn't know where to start. She squealed stomping her feet beneath the table to release the energy. Pictures, she'd start there.

Brione clicked on "Images." The pictures before her eyes made her lean into the monitor. There were mountains, valleys, glaciers, snow, a winter heaven. What had he done during his visit? Did he hike? Was he alone? Was it as cold as it appeared?

She grabbed her phone and went back to his contact. And she noticed the note, Call me and let's have dinner sometime. She had stared at it for most of her *non-effective* study time.

She could send a text.

Her fingers hovered over the screen. No. She shook her head, and then what? He'd text her back and want to talk on the phone. She put the phone back on the table. Music. That would help.

She stood and turned on the wireless speaker, stopping by the kitchen for some water. Back at the coffee table, she sat in front of her textbook. She untwisted the top off the plastic bottle and took a cool drink. She scanned her phone for some music, pressed play and turned back to the case.

Brione read through several immigration cases for class. Her doorbell rang and she glanced at the clock. She wasn't expecting anyone, she never had guests except... She stood up and walked to the door and glanced through the peephole. Her heart dropped to her feet. *What is he doing here?*

Stewart leaned into the doorbell. *Ding dong. Ding dong. Ding dong.*

"I know you're there. Open up and stop staring at me through the peephole."

Brione jerked back, placing her back against the door. She cracked her knuckles and exhaled a shaky breath. Her palms sweaty, she looked down at her t-shirt and leggings. Her clothes didn't matter. But she felt more in control in a suit. Less like the young woman that fell for his smile and honey-laced words only to get stung by a wasp.

"You can do this Bri," she whispered running her wet hands down her pants. She clutched one hand in the other to still her shaking limbs. "This is your space. You are in control."

Ding dong. Ding dong. Ding dong.

"I'm not leaving." He stated.

She placed a hand on the handle and unlocked the bolt. She peeked through the opening created by the chain. "What do you want?"

"I promise this is not the way you want to handle this situation." He leveled his deadly stare.

"I'm studying."

"I guess Kayla will call you next week then. Give you time to study." He stepped back never breaking eye contact with her. She unlatched the chain, stepping back as he strolled in like he owned the place.

Brione closed the door. Stewart was like the boogeyman. People refute its existence until it pops up under your bed.

He sat on the couch and leaned back. "Are you always this rude to your guests?" He stretched his arms across the cushions, obviously comfortable. "Can I get some water, sweet tea, a sandwich? Damn." He laughed at his own joke.

"You didn't drive to Houston for water or a sandwich. So stop with the dramatics. What do you want?"

"What I've always wanted, *you.*"

Stewart Bradley knew how to pop up on her doorstep when she felt confident, when she finally decided to not let him push her around, then he emerged from the shadows to call her bluff.

"Have a seat? I won't bite."

The invisible shackles clanked around her ankles as she sat in the chair closest to the door. "What do you want Stewart?"

"How are you?" His eyes scanned her body. She wrapped her arms protectively around her waist.

"I'm fine."

"When did you cut your hair and what's up with your clothes?"

"Stewart I'm studying." His mother was always dressed to perfection including a string of white pearls. He wanted a clone of Mrs. Bradley, the thought of her old sweats and short hair irking him brought a smile to her face. "And I like my bob."

"Is this how you're carrying yourself nowadays?"

"Is that why you visited? If so, we can end this conversation here and now." She swallowed hard.

"Don't let law school go to your head. This is still my show."

"Why don't you move on and let us move on too?"

"There is no *us* without me," he growled. "You got into law school because of me. You can't care for Kayla without a job. What about her education? Her tutors? Her nanny? And don't forget about your pops." His glare intimidating. "I will deliver his career in a wastebasket. Is that what you want? Do you want to ruin everyone's lives because of your selfishness?"

The boogeyman live and in living color. Panic was rioting inside her gnawing away at her confidence. Gnawing away at her plans and dousing her hope.

She once trusted this man and thought he loved her. That was the face of love. It was laughable. Her tongue felt thick and her nerves made it hard to form a coherent thought. She was tired of him pushing her around.

Don't let him push you around. Brione couldn't trust that voice, hadn't she invited him into her life in the first place. She dropped her head, stirring uneasily in the chair, hoping to hide the shame from his probing eyes. It was the cost of trusting an untrustworthy person. A person who valued self-ambition and greed over people. *How had I missed it?*

"Are you done playing with me?" His nostrils flared with fury.

She nodded, fear splintered her heart.

"Good." The storm clouds left his eyes. "Mom wants us to set a date."

She squeezed her eyes shut gripping the arms of the chair. "Stewart you don't want to marry me. We have nothing in common—"

"Nothing in common? We have *everything* in common. Let me shoot it to you straight. I want a date or so help me, Brione Allen, I'll bury you and your father's dreams of sitting in the Oval Office. And I'll ensure you never ever see our daughter again." He ground the words out through clenched teeth. "Understand?"

"Yes."

～

Continue Reading...

**Get Your Copy on Amazon
or Read in Kindle Unlimited!**

Ready for Love Boxed Set (Books 1 - 3)

Smith Pact Duo (Contemporary Romance)

Yuki's Luck (Book 1)

Tempting Asher (Book 2)

Smith Surprise (Book 3)

See all of my books on my website:

http://www.janesedixon.com/books.

Steamy
Sensations
HOLIDAY LOVE

10 Authors. 10 Holidays. 10 *Steamy Romances*.

Ten romance authors bring you a sexy story to fire up your holiday. Each author has their own series in 2019 with one thing in common - Holidays!

Check out all of the Steamy Sensations books HERE or my website janesedixon.com/steamy-sensations!

ABOUT THE AUTHOR

Ja'Nese Dixon pens tales of romance in several sub-genres. But her favorites are the ones that manage to keep readers sitting on the edge of their seats lying to themselves about reading "just one more chapter".

Ja'Nese is an avid reader and coffee drinker, who also loves to run, cook, and craft. Her ultimate goal as a writer is to give you a little "staycation" with every story. And she aims to make this present story no exception. Sit back, grab a snack and enjoy.

Ja'Nese calls Houston home with her husband, three kiddos and a four-legged diva dog.

Visit her website at www.janesedixon.com if you enjoy romance, suspense and good stories.

Subscribe to Ja'Nese Newsletter "Reader's Staycation" for reader exclusives, regular giveaways and more.

Stay in Touch:
www.janesedixon.com
info@janesedixon.com

facebook.com/AuthorJaNeseDixon

twitter.com/janesedixon

instagram.com/authorjanesedixon

amazon.com/author/janesedixon

bookbub.com/authors/ja-nese-dixon

ABOUT THE PUBLISHER

Purpose Prevails Publishing
2231B Center St. STE 144
Deer Park, TX 77536
www.purposeprevailspublishing.com